I0716943

A Powerhouse Novel

# Altair

L. J. Black

For Sae.

# Altair

I'm a stranger to myself now
The sadness has stolen my face
Every shred left is a farce
A demon pretending to be me

- Breska Liotson, "Depression"

# PROLOGUE

I choose Death.

I think I chose it a million times without realizing it. The bitter irony of my decisions fills me. My life opens up before me like a million-petal lotus revealing its core. I can't help but wonder what I would have been if I were ordinary. I can't help but wonder if I would have been given more time.

And time is against me now.

# PART 1

1

## *NOW*

The orange light of Widdershin's Sun burns deep red late in the day as it dips below the horizon. I watch through the yellow leaves of the alien trees as the light fades away and the blazing stars of night take over. Around me the nightlights of the quad slowly come on in a comforting rainbow of soft blues and greens. Across from me and to the right, transit squares flare up periodically as one by one Witches return home.

I sit waiting on a low wall in my usual place, away from the bustle of the Academy's classrooms and research halls. Turning my face upward, I catch the soft light of the turning galaxy above. The glorious bands of twinkling light slowly become visible in the darkening sky. If there is one thing I know for certain, the view is worth the journey here.

The air turns chilly around me. I am told that winter here is colder than any cold I have known. This strange little planet doesn't have the gentle seasons I was used to back in Georgia. But I knew that before coming here.

"Penny," a familiar voice calls out to me. I turn my face to the left, away from the transit squares, to find the source.

"Hello, Altair," I say.

"I hope I didn't startle you," he says.

"You didn't."

He smiles and sits facing me on the wall. I draw my knees up close to my chest and hug them. I watch Altair as he watches me back.

"I thought you might be out here," he says.

"Why?" I ask, not wondering why he thought he would find me here so much as wondering why he would bother to find me at all.

He shrugs. "Since the Academy is going on a break next week, I thought I would go back to my foster home. Are you returning to Earth?" he asks.

I shake my head in response. Anger flares in me. I haven't forgiven my family enough to set foot back on Earth. I swore I would never return.

"I'll be staying here," I say.

He shakes his head. "No," he says. "You should go somewhere, if only to take a mental break."

He is referring to my constant need to work since I got to Widdershin. And as a regular work partner, he often goes with me on my trips halfway across the galaxy. I have not paused once in five months since being here. I barely remember what it was like to be in school back on Earth and have all that free time. I barely remember the regular rhythm of eighth grade.

"It'll be October back on Earth," I say absently. I don't want to go back there. I would rather stay on Widdershin

Altair is silent. He looks across the quad in the direction of the transit squares. I follow his gaze and see the people coming in. Not one of them is human. Some humans are Witches, but humans are just not that common. I have become so accustomed to seeing alien faces that Altair's human features occasionally seem strange to me.

"You could come with me," he says suddenly.

I swivel my head around to look at him. He is serious, that much I can tell, but otherwise I can't discern what he's thinking. His dark brown eyes are impenetrable.

"Why?"

He shrugs again. "For company."

The light is fading quickly now, so I cannot quite make out

his expression. I think he is lonely, at least his voice would tell me that if he was from Earth. Altair is from so far away no amount of space travel can get him home. He is from next door, from another universe.

My family would never accept the existence of other universes, much less believe a human could be from one. I don't understand their views, but I think I have been away from Earth too long to understand Earth centric thinking anymore.

"How long would we be gone?" I ask.

"A few days, maybe the whole week," Altair responds. "You can do the requested power work in the area."

He is referring to the commission I have yet to accept in his neighborhood (by neighborhood, I mean galaxy). Altair is enticing me with work. He knows by now that it is my greatest weakness.

I roll my eyes. I couldn't care about anything else in the entire Universe. I only care about power now. I only care about being useful. I am stubborn and spiteful like that.

"I can't promise I'll be polite," I say, partly hoping to put him off and partly hoping to warn him.

Altair's mouth twitches in amusement. "I've told my foster family all about you."

I glare at him. As much as it bothers me that I have become bitter and resentful and even rude, irrationally it bothers me more that people know about it. But there's not much I can do. My reputation includes my difficulty. Most Witches or commissions don't care because they only care about what I can do. They only care about my power.

A thought crosses my mind and I ask the question before thinking better of it. "Is Ikthiel going to be around?"

Altair is not surprised by the words. It's also common knowledge that demons get along better with me (or maybe I with them). I used to be a nice person once. But that was before.

"I think he might be," Altair says.

Ikthiel, as a demon, is barred from ever setting foot on Widdershin. As an outsider and a transplant myself, I find this bizarrely unfair. I have sympathy for the demon where most would feel only resentment, dislike, or simply fear. I seldom see him, mostly when I am working on commissions. That's the only time I get off Widdershin these days.

I glance back across the quad and see the beautiful lights of the transit area come up. Where all the people blinked in and out only a little while ago, the gentle glow of transit squares illuminates the opposite end of the quad. I imagine myself going through them and never coming back. How can I be so unhappy here, in this place where *magic* is normal?

"All right, I'll come," I finally say to Altair. The sun has set behind him and I can see him properly now in the steady night-glow of the quad. He looks at me with his usual sad gaze.

"Good," he says. "We'll leave the day after tomorrow."

I smile for the first time all day, maybe all week. The smile feels genuine if unpracticed. Maybe it's the prospect of getting off this tiny planet that excites me.

Maybe it's the idea of going someplace that is somebody's *home.*

2

## *BEFORE*

The summer before high school, the Academy admitted me for the first time. If things had gone according to plan, I would have attended regular, human high school every year and returned to the Academy each summer. Then, upon graduation and freedom from my human obligations, I would have moved into the Academy's equivalent of college. Three years of training later and I could have come home.

But that is another life, not this one.

I stand in a hot, windless field outside Darien, Georgia. My mother or my father or *any* family should be with me. I stand alone about ten feet from my guardian. I have become a ward of the Witches. My family has abandoned me.

Part of me hates being a Witch. I feel responsible for things so far outside my control I should be absolved of them. I did not choose to have the Spark—the name the Witches give to the magic core. I did not choose to be different. It wasn't my choice to be born a Williams. I did not choose to be born into a line of silent Witches. My ancestors let go of the power a long time ago, hidden from even themselves since the time of the Salem madness.

And more than all of that insanity, I am NOT responsible for my family falling apart.

*I am NOT responsible.*

I swallow forcibly. I realize that I've been clenching my fists for the past ten minutes. For a second, I close my eyes, grateful I'm standing far enough ahead of my guardian that my face is not visible.

Steady again, I glance over my shoulder. "Are they late?" I ask.

Rebecca Whitney, an elderly Spent Witch assigned as my guardian, nods her head once. "There must be a delay."

I retreat again into my thoughts. I got an email from Lucy St. John yesterday. She is my best friend and despite my departure off-world I am trying to keep in contact with her. I can't tell her anything about where I am going or what I am doing, but it will be nice to have her there. In some sense, she is my last connection to Earth.

I had to lie to her about where I was going. I told her I was going to boarding school, which I suppose wasn't entirely a lie. She chose to interpret it as a human boarding school with a human curriculum.

Lucy had moved over to the local private school two years ago. She sometimes seemed years ahead of me in both her studies and in her maturity. Her feelings about going to private school reflected in how I feel about my power.

"It's awful being gifted," she had said. "It takes over your life. They want even more from you. And you can never give enough."

I have been feeling those same hooks of expectation since the discovery of my gift.

Three years have passed. Now that I am going, I am expected to live up to expectations. Not only am I gifted, but I am gifted in excess. No Witches in my family for centuries then I come along with more power than any living Witch and no explanation as to why. The thought intimidates me.

"They're coming now," Mrs. Whitney says, breaking my thoughts. Though she is older and her Spark has flamed out, she is still a Witch. Her power to see through the veil of reality is still there though much diminished.

Across the field I can just make out the three figures who appeared seemingly out of nowhere. I know two of them well from my training and the third I have met a few times since learning of my power three years ago. I expected only one of them to show up.

Mrs. Whitney's old woman's voice croaks out in surprise, "All three?" She lets out a tight breath and draws even with me. "Let's go," she says.

I pick up my backpack and we begin to cross the grass. The three figures come towards us now too. The woman and the boy are human enough, but my Witch's eyes can see through the illusion on the man. His name is Harilsen and when I blink I can see the alien under the human guise. Black skin, eyes solid slate gray with a white pupil, too many fingers, and no hair on his bald head: he is as alien to me as I am to him. He is one of my tutors, tasked with preparing me for the Academy. I know him well from my training the past few years and his appearance is no longer unusual to me

The woman is Alicia Cole, the main Academy liaison for Earth. She commutes back and forth so much I suspect she uses some power or spell matrix of her own to transport. She assesses me with cool gray eyes and a ghost of a smile. The day is hot and I can see her feeling it; she is originally from a planet markedly colder than Earth. A few million humans live amongst many sentient species there. My world opened up three years ago when my gift became known. I did not know about aliens or non-Earth humans or anything about planets back then. Now those gray eyes look at me, her dark hair bluish in tint with a feathering of gray hair just starting over her ears. The last I saw her four months ago when I became a ward of the Witches, the gray hair was not as apparent.

Alicia Cole turns to the boy and asks if there will be any problems lifting four of us off Earth or if she should make her own way back.

"It's no problem," the boy answers. His name is Altair Nebeck. He has accompanied every person who visited me from the Academy. He is also one of my tutors. Aside from his height well over six feet tall, his features are perfectly ordinary. Brown hair, brown eyes, and scrawny build.  He looks like most teenagers on Earth, like most boys around seventeen. As with most Witches, he has one, focused power. His is teleportation. No one in this universe has power like Altair's. But he is not from this universe.

"We should go," Alicia Cole says. "Our window will close in a few minutes."

I look back to Mrs. Whitney and thank her. Then I look around me and take in the sky and the grass and the view. I soak in the image of my home planet one last time. My family rejected the reality of me when my power came to light. My vision of home vanished in only a few years.

I turn away from the view and step closer to Altair. He places a hand on my shoulder and Harilsen and Alicia Cole link to him as well. I glance around one last time, adjust my backpack, and then look up at Altair who stands a head and shoulders taller than me.

The blue sky of Earth haloing him blacks out to the darkness between spaces.

The sturdy ground beneath my feet fades as I say goodbye to Earth for the last time.

3



## *NOW*

Orange. Why is everything always *orange?*

Altair's foster home is on this ancient planet in an ancient galaxy far from the Milky Way. By my perspective this galaxy is at the edge of the universe. Of course, from here it seems that Earth is at the edge of the universe.

The ancient M-type star is a sad flickering light sinking towards the horizon. The atmosphere colors an orange hue on this old world. Earth is about 4.5 billion years old. The universe is, rounding up, roughly 13.8 billion years old. This star has lived since the time of the first stars. This planet formed some 13.6 billion years ago and took its time cooling as I understand it.

The first sentient species on this planet—a silicon-based creature the size of a mouse—lived in such ancient time that I can barely fathom it. The current natives of the planet are by all counts the fifth sentient species to populate this place. I do not understand why Altair's foster family are reptilian hexapods with four eyes and opposable thumbs, but he seems to view them fondly. I have tried in the two days I have been here to understand that affection and be kind to them as well. Today, however, I am standing very close to the edge of the cliff, a good distance from their expansive home.

The view reminds me of places on Earth. The landscape is

the kind you would see in old Westerns, the ones that were filmed in Monument Valley back in the day. The campy ones.

One thing I have come to appreciate about the universe is the way you can find parallels everywhere. Even this far away from the familiar, I can see a bit of Earth in this stark landscape. For a moment I feel as if I haven't really left Earth after all. I watch the red sun sink below another monument bringing twilight to the valley. True sunset is a few hours away yet. In the dimness the lights of the homes all around, on top of the monuments and in the flatlands below, blink on populating the area with fireflies in shades of blue. The unexpected color is enough to remind me this is not Earth.

This is Kaldreesa.

Breathing the air here feels like Earth, feels like Widdershin, feels like a half-dozen other worlds. Some places I had to be inoculated prior to the trip to help breathe the air better. Other places I wear a portable atmosphere. But here the mixture is similar enough to Earth to fool my lungs. This must be half the reason Altair lives here. He is just as human as I am.

I crouch down in the gravel, hugging my knees and continuing to watch the sunlight fade. Overhead the stars twinkle into view. Behind me the gravel crunches.

"Does our view please?"

I look up to my right and meet the yellow eyes of Altair's foster mother, Imfra-Rega. "Yes," I answer. I manage a weak smile. "It reminds me of parts of Earth."

She blinks at me and says, "I would think the reminder would not please you."

I feel anger at the memory her words bring. I stare into her eyes feeling the seething rage I've worked to suppress for months. My family turned their backs on me. And they blamed me for the breakup of our house. This mother from a different world, from a different species, found it in herself to take in Altair for his time here. I blink and turn away, feeling the rage-tears rising behind my eyes.

Imfra-Rega places her first foreclaw on my shoulder. I have in the past pushed people away for doing that. I dislike the pity and the sympathy. I want to be left to grieve in peace. I hate it when others borrow my grief to feel grief of their own. I have lost almost everything in such a short amount of time. Darkness wells up inside me and tries to consume me almost daily.

But the part of me that is still my former self cannot push this loving mother away. She has had twelve of her own children and Altair is not even the fifth foster they have taken in. How is there any fairness in the universe if kind souls like this exist in the same space as harsh individuals like my family?

My hands begin to shake as I lose control for the first time in almost six months.

Imfra-Rega crouches behind me and wraps her tail around and hugs me to her bulky chest. She rocks me the way I saw her rock her own offspring when one of them was afraid of the lightning storm. She wipes my tears as much as she can and whispers, "We hold you safely." I hear her whisper that to her children. I wonder about the cultural context.

My whole body shudders like a leaf as I cry onto this gentle alien's rough chest. She does not let me go for a long time. It takes me a while to just feel the pain I have been ignoring. Only when I am quiet and have stopped sobbing does she gently let me go. The sky is dark now punctuated only by the brightest stars. Here in the deepest depths of space surrounded by pure darkness, those pinpricks of light give me hope.

"We should feed you," Imfra-Rega says softly.

I nod and look up at her.

She answers before I ask, "You look like yourself." More than anything the stain of crying is too difficult to explain.

No one can control these kinds of feelings. I get hit by them for no reason and with no real provocation. Having to explain that repeatedly is just painful and undesirable. So I have taken to suppressing them.

Together we walk back to the house where I can see the family waiting inside. They have no exterior walls to the main living area. Kaldrasticans do not require furniture the way humans do. Their living space is mostly just an open room with a sunken area for eating and a raised area for the children to play on. Two of Imfra-Rega's children are still young enough to live at home. The others have all grown and moved on.

I perch on the edge of the sunken area and watch the family gather together for their evening meal. Altair enters from across the space, sees me, and makes his way around the cluster of Kaldrasticans. He sits next to me with no more greeting than a thin smile and hands me a small electronic device that, if I'm honest, resembles a smartphone.

"The group requesting your power assistance made contact with the local office here," he explains. "It seems they did not want to disturb you when you are on break."

I sigh and scroll through the information on the screen. It processes like a smartphone too, only much faster. "Am I really that much of a pain to deal with?" I ask bitterly. I already know the answer is yes, but sometimes I feel the need to ask.

Altair looks at me seriously and answers, "You can be. But I don't think you do it on purpose."

Studying his gaze, I wonder why he gives me the benefit of the doubt when so many others deign not to try. "You don't," I say. A question and a statement.

He shrugs. "Some of us have had hard lives," he says. "But not everyone understands that."

I stare at him, for the first time wondering what happened in his past that he can make such an observation. Why does he live with a foster family? What led him to coming into our universe in the first place? I suddenly remember his home is so far away that no amount of space travel or portals can make the trip. How does one become an exile from their own universe?

Not for the first time I close myself to the questions I could ask. I look away. I am so wrapped up in my own grief and my own lack of human contact that the thought of asking someone else personal questions seems ludicrous.

"I'll contact them first thing tomorrow," I say instead. Despite my difficulty, I am not in the habit of keeping people waiting. I always feel it's better to get things done in a timely manner rather than loiter about waiting.

Altair only nods in response. Imfra-Rega calls us down to eat and we both scoot off the ledge to join the family on the floor. We eat the same food as our hosts, the nutritional needs being similar enough that we don't generally have to worry about poisoning ourselves.

I chew on leaves oddly resembling kale and marvel again at the parallels I find in the universe.

4

***BEFORE***

A few weeks before I turned thirteen, my family decided they didn't want me in their house anymore. They didn't want a Witch in the family.

When my situation changed, they assigned me to the custody of the Witch living nearest to Darien. Mrs. Whitney lived in Wyoming and drove cross country to Darien. She moved her old RV into the park right off I-95. I moved in with her in January, right before my thirteenth birthday. The Witches handled my transfer paperwork to make it look like I was leaving McIntosh Middle School at the will of my parents. In a sense I was, but I wasn't transferring to another school like they thought.

Sometimes I go for a walk in the evening. It's not the safest thing this close to the interstate, but I rarely if ever make it past the outdoor eating area by the Burger King. I usually buy a milkshake or some French fries and just sit for a while thinking. Mrs. Whitney has given me a small allowance, something that my parents never did.

Late in April about a week before I leave Earth, I find myself making that familiar walk and buying those generic French fries and milkshake again so I can sit and watch the sun setting.

Today, like so many times before, I am not alone sitting on

that concrete patio.

"Ikthiel," I say, greeting the familiar demon. He takes a seat across from me and steals a French fry. He has not, in four months, paid once.

"How are you?" he asks.

I once scolded him for not asking me that on a particularly bad day. That was two years ago. He has asked me how I am doing every time he has seen me since.

"I'm doing alright," I answer. I glance back into the Burger King and note the group of teenagers watching us. Two of the girls and one of the guys seem overly interested in Ikthiel. "What do you look like to them?" I ask.

Ikthiel smiles, glances at the teens who promptly look away, and answers, "Oh, I'm very attractive to most people."

I roll my eyes. Not much surprises me with Ikthiel anymore. I've known him long enough to say that. Then again, I can see the real Ikthiel.

"So, what brings you out here?" I ask, taking a fry and dunking it in my vanilla shake.

Ikthiel watches as I eat the sweetened potato, but answers, "You're leaving next week. I won't be able to visit as often at the Academy."

I make a face at his words. I already know this of course, but it still seems unfair. Just because Ikthiel is a demon, just because he is not like the rest of the Witches, he's banned from Widdershin. Not just the Academy, but the whole planet Widdershin. It doesn't matter that he's working *with* the Witches and has been for decades or longer, he's still banned. He is as much an outsider as I am in the Witch's world. And as such I am careful to keep my relationship with Ikthiel secret. It is frowned upon to be friends with a demon. It is against Witch regulation to form an alliance with them. I have done both.

"So where will you go to get your French fries?" I ask sarcastically.

He raises his eyebrows and glances back at the Burger King window. "I could always ask them."

I snort. I'm sure the local teen population would back away

quickly if they found out what Ikthiel really is. He should unsettle me, but his presence is comforting. He is proof of something bigger in the universe, despite that proof being simplistic evil.

"I will try to be present though," he continues. "I do enjoy your company for some reason, and I would like to continue it."

That's as close to a compliment as Ikthiel gets. "I like you, too," I answer.

He gets a wicked look in his eye. "I don't think it should be difficult for us to see each other if you are working."

"No, I'm sure you're right about that," I say. We already discussed the possibility of taking commissions abroad. He suggested it as a means for making me independent and as a way for us to communicate. Demons are often called in to facilitate some Witchwork. I couldn't predict ahead of time whether he would be called, but my previous interactions with him, the ones the Witches knew about, would certainly make him a priority contact. After all, without Ikthiel, I would never have been discovered.

Around me the sky has dimmed to a pinkish orange and the patio lights have come on. The group of teens inside seems to be finishing up. I should head back before it becomes too dark.

"I'll walk you back," Ikthiel offers. He glances over his shoulder at the Burger King window and says, "You should hear what they think about you. I don't particularly care for it."

I shrug. "I can hear it if I want to, but I prefer not to," I say. "I don't hold people responsible for their thoughts. Only their actions."

"You're more generous than some species."

He isn't joking. I have become much better at controlling my thoughts since hearing of such places.

We are about to walk off the patio when he pauses. Ikthiel offers his hand to me and I take it instinctively. I've held his hand before; it is the only compassion he was capable of in the beginning. His claws once gave me pause, but now I barely pay attention to them.

Together we walk down 251 and head across the interstate

toward Mrs. Whitney's home. Lights come on around us as we walk toward the RV park. Ikthiel stops near the entrance, just between the McDonald's and the main drive into the park.

He turns to me in the dimness and says, "I will do my best to break the rules."

"All right," I say. "I won't see you again before I go?"

"No," he says bluntly. "I have to go out to the Edge when I leave here. I won't return for a while."

He has told me this before so it comes as no surprise. But it still seems odd in some way as if it's the parting of friends.

"Be careful amongst the Witches," he says. "Be careful who you trust."

Whether he says that because he is a demon or because he is sincerely concerned for my safety, I'm not sure. I just know that I can trust him. I've been able to trust him all along.

"I'll be careful."

He moves to hug me. Surprised, I embrace this unusual friend. Rarely does he succumb to human sentiment. Then it is over. A moment later Ikthiel has vanished like fog in sunlight.

I walk into the RV park alone.

5



*NOW*

"Miss Williams," the Head Witch greets me. "Thank you for coming."

I nod curtly and try to swallow my aversion to being thanked. It takes a great deal of self-control to keep from blurting out some nasty remark. It's pointless to say it, but they only value my sheer power. The fact that they put up with my reputation for callousness only proves that. I feel no inclination to be kind.

I arrived only a few minutes ago. Altair gave me a transport spell to take me to this remote solar system at the edge of a galaxy at the end of the universe from Earth's perspective. Out here the galaxies move faster than conceivable and possess age beyond what Earth humans suspect. And this place is beautiful.

This oldest of places is a paradise of green and gold and brown and air so toxic I use not just power but technology to protect myself. A metal collar around my neck reminds me of the hostile environment and houses the personal atmosphere clinging to my skin. But the inconvenience is worth it. I have come to realize I collect views the way some people collect stamps. The knife-sharp mountains of this world, the razor cut canyons to my right, and the expansive vistas before me populated with an advanced urban center side-by-side with primitive forests: the latest view added to my collection.

All worlds are beautiful. And all are devastating in their beauty.

I glance at the pinkish-red sky and only momentarily glance at the sun. The aging red giant approaches the end of its lifetime. It has been lazy of late, puffing out its outer layers in waves that could level this last planet in this solar system. Its name, Velnu, means "the Last" in their language.

This rugged planet is home to several trillion people, the far distant horizons giving away its size. It may be similar to Earth, or similar to a rocky planet, but it is not home.

"Have you caught up on the project?" the Witch asks.

I look at him full on for the first time.

"You're doing a hydrostatic balancing and energy redirection of Solus there," I say in answer to the Witch's question. I can't remember his name and frankly it doesn't matter anyway. He is from this system, though most of the team had to be brought in from the surrounding areas.

I continue, "You're installing a temporary patch to stabilize the helium fusion and buy enough time for species relocation."

This kind of project is routine for Witches. This is the first one I have participated in.

"Correct," the Head Witch answers. The Witch's voice is scratchy, but I do expect that from a species that looks like a cross between a lizard and a chicken—feathers and all. One of four fore-claws points to the holographic display before us and manipulates it for a moment. The floating image of Solus rotates and zooms accordingly.

I've already lost interest. My gaze wanders around the room as they continue to go over the particulars of the project. I only have one job and that is to be a major power generator for the project. I'm often affectionately (or grudgingly) known as a "powerhouse."

This conference room—my only name for it—is large and rather ornate. Unlike Earth's Corinthian columns, the bas-relief carvings of the stone walls resemble some obsessive compulsive mathematician's desire for perfect angles. Some of the designs I recognize as fractal patterns, though I really don't know anything about them. The perfect sand-colored walls to my left and right frame enormous panoramic windows with thick glass of some polycarbonate material. I look again at the rugged and yet beautiful landscape and cityscape before me. Where Earth's cities would be constructed of metal and glass, their cities are constructed of stone and resin. I can see the movement of the city below us even from here. And I wonder what this civilization thought about having to leave this place and relocate.

"When will the demon arrive?" another of the Witches asks. These people don't really have genders as I understand them, or rather they have so many genders I am unable to classify them in human terms.

Their words about a demon immediately catch my attention. I understand that overcoming the natural degradation of entropy in this project is difficult and as such recruiting a natural rule-breaker like a demon is often useful. It hadn't occurred to me to think about whom I would be working with.

"Ikthiel hasn't arrived yet, though he should be here before we begin," the Lead Witch responds. "He is reliable and—," glancing at me, adds, "—he has worked with our powerhouse before."

Part of me feels relieved to know that Ikthiel is the demon. At least it is a familiar demon and not a stranger I would be working with.

As if right on cue, an attendant steps through the archway behind me and says, "Pardon me, Proirotr, but the demon Ikthiel has arrived."

I roll my eyes at the universe and its sense of humor. I turn around just in time to see the demon step through the doorway without waiting to be invited. My mouth twitches into the only semblance of a smile I have had all day.

"Good," the Proirotr says. The attendant leaves so quickly that I wonder if Ikthiel makes all creatures nervous. "Thank you for coming."

Ikthiel does not answer but merely nods at me in recognition. He stands next to me but doesn't say a word. I look him up and down, realizing he's wearing a light form of demon's armor. I can see the faint glistening of the power sewn into the seams of his clothes. I doubt anyone would notice it really. If I were on Earth, I would call the clothing leather, but out here it has nothing to do with cowhide. The effect is the same and the seams are blinking with the power infusing them.

Ikthiel catches me staring and he gives me a faint smile.

"Where are you coming from?" I ask.

"Someplace far away and unsafe."

His cryptic response tells me enough. Demons wear armor when they are surrounded by hostiles. I don't know what he gets up to during his free time. Most of the time I don't care enough to know. But today my curiosity is piqued by his attire.

I think he knows I'm actually curious for once because he adds, "We'll talk about it later."

I nod at him once and turn back to the display in front of us. None of the Witches are paying attention to us. We're the hired labor here. Back on Earth I would barely be in high school. Out here I'm a respected member of society, even if I have a difficult reputation.

The meeting concludes and I draw my attention back to the Head Witch. The Proirotr signals for the group to leave. A transit square lights up on the floor at the east side of the room. It's large enough for all of us to step through.

Transit spells like this are common in the universe, though they have gotten more efficient since Altair crossed over. His unusual method of instantaneous transport makes it possible to jump incredible distances with a smaller energy requirement than before. So I find myself blinking briefly as the personal atmosphere adjusts to our sudden displacement to one of the planet's moons. The near-vacuum of space surrounds us and the shielding works to compensate.

All around us the rocky moonscape is in shadow, but to my right, maybe a quarter mile in the distance, the day-night line approaches. Beyond that point is Solus and our job. The moon turns us toward the dayside, taking us closer to our work.

I glance at Ikthiel standing next to me and realize for the first time that he requires no atmosphere out in the depths of space.

Is it just because he is a demon? Or is there some trick to existing in a vacuum for long periods?

He catches me staring and the corner of his mouth twitches for a moment. Then we both turn our attention back to the Proirotr and wait for instructions as we begin.

In the smallest, deepest part of my ear, I hear the Head Witch's scratchy voice calling out the parts of the spell as each of us steps forward. Witches largely have one or two talents (the record is five in one person, but that was a long time ago). Our abilities vary as widely as the species we come from and each of us plays a role. Here our combined uniquenesses work together as one. The Lead Witch orchestrates our combined efforts, hopefully to help slow the sun's catastrophic end.

The dawn breaks and Solus rises to my right. I lift a hand to my eyes and recall the shielding, a kind of "virtual sunglasses," I had taken the time to emplace just above my eyebrows. The visor snaps back into reality, becomes necessarily opaque, and I let my hand drop to my side again. The rest of the Witches have done the same or something similar, though Ikthiel's version has turned his eyes blood red.

From up here in space, this close to all things and without the disruption of the atmosphere below, Solus is entrancing. The red-orange-pink hues circulate, seething across the surface in an agitated way. If I had to judge the character of the star, I would call it a cranky old man. A cranky old man telling us to get off his lawn. The star is slowly dying.

All these farthest out planets should have disappeared a billion years ago when the helium flash destroyed the innermost planets. Certainly this whole system became uninhabitable for a while. But life made its way again and the people who live here are actively choosing not to succumb to the previous system's fate. The species has been making preparations for millennia in anticipation of no longer having their homeworld. It is a sad fate to no longer have a home. They refused to accept oblivion.

In five billion years will the human race choose the same thing?

The Witches and Ikthiel and I form a loose ring as Solus rises above us. The Proirotr makes no move that I can see, but I feel him bring to life a spell matrix more complex than any I have ever seen. In five months of time working commissions as a power Witch, this is the most delicate job I have ever been asked to fuel. The matrix is a blue-golden hued geodesic sphere floating in the space between us, each vertex a node for a Witch's power.

I watch as Witch after Witch emplaces their power in the matrix. There are eight of us including the Proirotr and Ikthiel. Each Witch's power falls into the matrix and lights up a significant portion of the sphere. The spell matrix will enact when all eight of us have placed our power in it. I go last after Ikthiel to give the spell as much strength as is necessary to complete its purpose.

I have done this many times, but never with this much intricacy. I am not nervous. Nerves went away a long time ago. The only reality of having enormous power is the confidence it grants you. Confidence escaped me on Earth. Out here I feel no hesitation.

Ikthiel steps forward next to me and places his clawed hand on the node closest to him. His power seeps from him in a bleeding pool of red light contaminating the spell matrix with its glow. The power is familiar to me, but two of the experienced Witches across from me visibly react to its presence. Demon's power, while kin of Witch's power, often makes Witches uncomfortable with its twisting, perversions of reality. It is exactly those characteristics needed for this work today.

As the red power sinks deeply into the matrix, Ikthiel steps back and looks at me with his usual mixture of amusement and expectation. I nod at him once and step forward for my part.

My node is a simple, glowing sphere devoid of any of the complex lines at the others' parts. I am simply here to fuel the mess. My power need not be controlled now that the matrix is nearly complete. I can simply lay as much as necessary into the matrix and it will run.

I place my palm up to the node and it lights up in blinding white. My power is familiar to me by now and I can see through the light to what lies beneath. Around me I feel the other Witches recoiling at the power's influx. Ikthiel alone takes a step forward and places a clawed hand at my back. As a demon he is very attracted to my power. But even now when I am extremely vulnerable, all my attention focused on the matrix, I feel no fear and Ikthiel does nothing but support me as I brace myself against the tide of power.

The intricate lines of the geodesic dome burn white against the dark of space and the rose red of Solus. I feel the spell begin to take and let my hand fall to my side, taking a step back into Ikthiel's hand. He places the clawed hand on my shoulder and we and the Witches turn our faces upward as the matrix rises away from us.

In the vast space between the moon and Solus, the matrix expands exponentially until it is larger than Solus itself. It has receded enough into the distance that it seems smallish from here, but even so the detail is apparent as the geodesic dome unfolds and wraps itself around Solus's shivering form. Though we are millions of miles from the edges of Solus, this planet having been the original farthest from the old sun, we can still feel the shudder of spacetime around us as the deteriorating star suddenly stabilizes. Though none of it is truly tangible, the twisting of spacetime feels like the fingers of a harpist strumming across still strings. I feel the vibration of it in my soul and wonder for a moment if it is only because I am attached to the spell. But I do not have the time to think of such things now.

"It took," the Proirotr says.

A general air of relief settles on the group as we all blink and come back to the reality around us. I breathe deeply and feel my atmosphere adjusting around me.

The Proirotr and the other Witches are speaking to one another and I turn to Ikthiel who only now pulls his hand away.

"Where were you?" I ask. Though we are on a barren moon and there are certainly better things to speak about, this is the question bothering me.

Ikthiel smiles and says quietly, "I was out at the Edge, that place I told you about." I recall his story about the empty place where he goes sometimes. It is a place where the neighboring universe is pressing in on ours, where the realities are fighting not the blend. He told me in this place that he is sometimes a human, sometimes a Witch, sometimes a demon, and sometimes all three. Reality is fluid and conflicting out there.

"Where was it this time?" I ask. Its physical location in our universe migrates, not always able to stay in place.

"Not far from here," Ikthiel answers. "I will take you out there."

The Proirotr calls our attention before I get to answer. In the space between one breath and the next, we are transported en masse back to the planet's surface. I look around myself, touch the life-support collar briefly, and blink in the light of Solus. The hues of the planet have shifted in the slight change in the light. We took enough time settling before coming back that the sun has become more orange in color. Again with the orange.

I turn to Ikthiel who is looking at me expectantly. "I'm sorry, did you say something?" I ask. For half a second I realize it's the first time I've apologized for anything in months.

Ikthiel's mouth twitches into what I assume is an amused smirk. "I asked if you were planning to return to Kaldreesa right away."

I blinked and said, "I hadn't really considered. Did you have something in mind?"

He nods. I realize the other Witches are oblivious to our conversation. It's not the first time Ikthiel has shielded our conversations from eavesdropping. It was a regular occurrence back home.

He pauses, seems to think for a moment, and asks as if the words are difficult, "Would you please come with me to the Edge? I believe it would be educational for you to see the universe out there. While you are in the neighborhood, so to speak."

His phrasing takes me aback for a moment. Ikthiel rarely if ever makes requests. He is always courteous to me and something bordering on kind. I have long suspected my power is what makes him so respectful. The look on his face suggests sincerity, but again I can't be sure if it's his demonself twisting truth to get what he wants. I have always been safe with Ikthiel, safer than with my family and even than with the Witches.

"All right," I say. "I will go with you."

I hear the words of the Witches coming back to my ears now. Ikthiel takes the time to say goodbye and I do the same. The Proirotr thanks me, but I only feel indifference as usual.

"Are you ready?" Ikthiel whispers.

"Yes."

One clawed hand wraps around my wrist and the reality around us goes black.

6



*NOW*

Light hits me and my eyes wince in reaction to the strength. I blink a few times, feel Ikthiel's hand around my wrist, and steady myself. I have learned not to show weakness amongst demons, even in front of Ikthiel. They have no respect for weakness.

Ikthiel waits, but I signal him that I'm fine. We made a significant jump to get this far. Altair's teleportation routines technically break the laws of physics in this universe, so it can be a bit rough to make a jump using them. I don't usually make jumps this far without at least one pause part way along. Ikthiel it seems has adjusted to the difficulty.

Below my feet is a rocky surface. Beyond that basic observation, there is little to say about it. I do not recognize its composition or source.

"Where are we?" I ask.

"Rogue planetoid, far beyond any solar system or sun," Ikthiel answers. I look into the distance where the foreshorten horizon gives way to a spectacular vista of empty space and roiling galaxies. I don't recognize any of them, but I wouldn't expect to this far out.

"Is this the Edge?" I ask.

Ikthiel points a single claw in the direction ahead of us. "Just over there the realities begin to cross."

"I don't notice any difference," I say. The emptiness is consistent and absolute in all directions around us.

"You wouldn't notice it until you are right in it," he says. I look at him and he nods. He begins to walk in the direction he pointed. I follow a few steps behind.

The change is subtle. I don't realize we are in it until I look up and see that Ikthiel himself has changed. At one point he reaches a hand behind himself towards me and I see the claws are gone. He is as human as I am. Then he turns his face and his features have warped only a few steps later. The reality has distorted again and changed what he is.

Ikthiel glances back at me. He is no longer a human, he is a demon again. Just that quickly, from one breath to the next, he is different. Change is always like that, I suppose.

He reaches back to me and I take his clawed hand as it morphs again into tamer human fingers. We walk a little further into the Edge and I feel secure—as I usually do—with my demon guide.

The only solid thing I am connected to is his hand. All around and in ways I cannot describe reality shifts and warps and intrudes like the pressing of water on stone. My universe seems as solid as granite or marble or diamond, but if there's anything I've learned in my time away from Earth it's this: with enough time all things change, all things slip away. Here in this place where the basic rules of physics don't seem to apply, I watch through the lens of the Edge as stars implode and explode through a cycle of birth and death that reverses itself as quickly as it starts. I watch a passing galaxy reverse itself from a loose elliptical form back to the tightly packed spiral of its youth. This should not be possible of course, and would not be if not for where we are.

Even the air seems out of sorts, seems strange. Or maybe it's my personal atmosphere that is warped by the strangeness of existence.

"You should learn to breathe without assistance," Ikthiel comments. He must have either heard my thoughts about my atmosphere or have noticed me breathing differently.

"But I need air to survive," I answer. Sometimes I wonder what demons think.

"You only think you do," he replies.

I'm about to respond when I remember his lack of an atmosphere out at the moon over Velnu. "Wait," I say, "do you *need* an atmosphere?"

He turns around at looks at me, perfectly human and no claws digging into my hand. Then it clicks. At this moment he's *human*. As human as I am. Shouldn't he need something?

"Now you got it." He's clearly listening to my thoughts again.

I raise my eyebrows in surprise. "Okay, we'll save that talk for later."

I look around me again, at the planetoid below my feet that both is and is not there.

"Is this what you wanted me to see?" I ask.

"Partly," Ikthiel answers. Demons are rarely forthcoming.

"Then what?"

I realize he's staring at me.

"*What?*" I ask, hostility seeping in. I get stared at frequently.

"Are you still yourself?"

The question seems wrong somehow. Insane almost. But it's the right question. "Yes," I say. The answer is surprising.

I watch the demon-human-Witch-somethingelse watch me back. He is changing almost too rapidly for me to track the changes. I hold up our linked hands so I can see the fingers changing. My hand remains unchanged. His hand goes through form after form without pause. I mentally shove aside the questions I have on what other forms he is changing into and instead focus on the vital question.

"Why am I not changing?"

For a moment Ikthiel seems to have an answer. Then the demon-human-whatever eyes drop their all-knowing guise and the truth surfaces: "I don't know."

"I should be though, shouldn't I?"

"Everyone else does," Ikthiel answers. "At least, everyone else who's come with me. Even Altair, though he isn't from this universe."

Words fail me. Ikthiel doesn't need a response from me. I continue to hold onto his hand for security and watch my free hand remain stable amidst the chaos of this intrusive space. It's unsettling to watch the one stable thing in a landscape that is rapidly changing.

"We can get out over there," he says, gesturing in a seemingly random direction.

What feels like moments but could be longer, we come to a point on the planetoid where the ground has solidified before us. The surface at our feet still shifts in the changing realities, but there is a point where the chaos no longer reigns. Together we cross through the dividing line.

Our hands still clasped, I realize Ikthiel is a demon again and I am still myself.

Over my shoulder I can remotely see the place where we entered the Edge. It must be two miles or more from where we stand. It is as Ikthiel described: the Edge moves.

"Look," Ikthiel says.

I follow his gaze upward and see what he means me to see— maybe the real reason I'm out here.

At the Edge out in space, the boundary is more difficult to discern. I squint and strain my sight, but find I don't need to do that as I scan along the Edge. Some distance out into space, the Edge's boundary puckers and forms a funnel of sorts. This funnel is a broken point, a tear possibly. I can see something swarming at the Edge, something seething beyond the dividing lines of my own reality.

"What is that?" I ask Ikthiel.

When a minute passes and he doesn't answer, I look at him. He is as fixated on the roiling violation of spacetime as I am.

"What is it?" I whisper.

He looks at me, a glint of concern in his eyes. He would never show fear, but this is the closest I had ever seen. "I don't know," he says for the second time.

We look again on that seething shape—or shapes really. A tentacled mass of darkness, perhaps constructed of energy but nothing I recognize, fills my vision with darkness so deep my vision does not comprehend it. A feeling seeps into me so gradually I don't notice until it has numbed my limbs: dread.

"What do they want?" I ask, my heart quickening.

"How do you know it's a 'they'?" he asks.

"I don't know. Just a feeling, I think."

Ikthiel is looking at me when I turn to him.

"What?"

"Your perceptions are cleaner than mine," he explains, "less tainted by your own expectations. If you think it is a 'they', then it probably is."

Alarm jerks my head back to space and I realize the importance of the Edge. If this is a place where another universe encroaches upon our own, if this is a place where reality bends and shifts of its own volition, then what's to stop something from pushing through into our universe? What could stop something from tearing the division down? And would our universe even withstand such a tearing of the fabric of which it is made?

"I think we should worry," I say.

One glance at Ikthiel's face tells me he is listening to my thoughts again. Not just listening, but really believing them. In my surprise at how completely he trusts me, I let my guard down and I catch what I recognize to be his train of thought. For just a moment I hear him think, *I'll have to ask the others*. And when he thinks "others," the tone suggests he is thinking of other demons.

He hears me following his thoughts and his mouth twitches as he says, "You didn't think my only friends were humans and Witches?"

I snort. "No," I say. "But are demons really friends?"

"I would think you would know the answer to that already," he says with his eyebrows raised. He means himself to me, of course. I roll my eyes. "But I doubt you would classify my relationship with my colleagues as 'friendship'," he adds.

"Fair enough."

"Let me take you back," he says. "Are you returning to Kaldreesa?"

"Yes."

"I will set you back there."

I take a couple deep breaths out in this far-off space and brace myself for the return trip. Kaldreesa is almost twice the distance from here to Velnu. I nod at Ikthiel, who smirks at my expense. This time instead of grabbing my wrist, he doesn't let go of my hand.

Before I take another breath, the planet disappears around us.

The air on Kaldreesa feels dry in contrast to Velnu. I drop my atmosphere, letting go of the last remnants remaining after contact with the Edge. Ikthiel courteously left me on the plateau near Imfra-Rega's home. The piercing brightness of the afternoon sun permeates everything. Though the star is small and old, I still find the light bright for its age. Maybe I have been on Widdershin too long and I don't remember the brightness of an active star.

For a moment I just breathe and watch the view. I stand roughly where I sat earlier in the week, close to the edge of the plateau. Only now, the light is brighter and the vista before me buzzes with activity. Kaldrasticans preserved their heritage as much as possible. That being said, they still employ the convenience of space-faring technology. Below me in the valley, glittering in the afternoon light, shuttles akin to Earth's ground-based bus system ferry Kaldrasticans to and fro between the various plateaus. The ships are massive by my standards, but so are most Kaldrasticans. A human would see no need to make a ship that large.

Slowly, I let my breathing return to normal and my heart slow into calmness. The unnerving feeling of being at the Edge coupled with the mass of *something* waiting just on the other side—being back here feels like waking from a bad dream. Only somewhere out there the dream is reality.

"I am going across the valley if you would like to join me."

I turn to see Imfra-Rega approaching from the house. Behind her I can just make out the empty living quarters. The youngest children are no doubt still in school for the afternoon.

"Where are you going?" I ask.

My mind is still heavily on the images I faced out at the Edge, the roiling boil of space seething with something behind it. But it is too much to contemplate at the moment.

"To pick up food."

My stomach grumbles at the thought of food. I haven't eaten much today. And what energy I had from breakfast is long gone after working on Velnu. Fortunately, Ikthiel shouldered the energy burden of jumping back and forth to the Edge. I'm not sure if he does that from kindness or showing off.

My wrist communicator buzzes and I remember in that moment I have messages to answer.

"I think I'll stay here," I say to Imfra-Rega, "if you don't mind." The politeness is belated, but at least I remembered it.

"As you please," Imfra-Rega says. "I'll be home before dinner."

She gives my shoulder a squeeze with her foreclaw and turns in the direction of the nearest shuttle station about a mile or so across the plateau. For a moment I watch her walk away, then I turn and head for the steps of the home. There I perch and take a moment to unfold my wrist communicator into something the size of an Earth tablet. A few buttons later and I have a look at the message list waiting for me.

A little ways down, buried under the pile of job requests I haven't reviewed yet, are two messages. One is from Rebecca Whitney, her regular communication that comes through about once a week. I was only in her care for a few months, but she has maintained contact with me despite my inability to regularly message her back.

The second message comes from Lucy St. John. The communicator picks up messages from every social media profile and email platform I had back on Earth, so sometimes the messages are short. This time the message is longer and has a few pictures. This one I open first.

**To: Penelope Williams**
**From: lsj.fish**

**(via Google Offworld Exchange)**
Hi Penny,

I hope you are doing well. Your last message made it sound like your studies were difficult but you're being treated well at least. So that's good. I hope that's true and you're not just making me feel better.

I miss hanging out with you. I hope you can come home on your time off. I feel like I never get to see you.

The news is your parents' divorce finalized. I don't know if you had heard about that, or if they are even talking to you right now. I never understood why they were so mean to you. I'm glad you were sent to live with your great-Aunt because at least she was nice. You should just get emancipated from your family. That's what my mom says. Then you can live with us if you want.

Anyway, miss you millions. Here are some pictures of me at the Tennessee Aquarium. You know I love that place.
Hugs and kisses,
Lucy

The pictures make me smile. Lucy hams it up taking selfies with various fish and has a hilarious face in one where she is touching a stingray. She's always loved fish. Her mother is a biologist and has indulged this. A couple times a year they make the trip up to Chattanooga to visit Lucy's favorite fish. A few of those times they managed to snag a behind-the-scenes tour with her mother's marine biology friends.

The second message is from Rebecca Whitney and reads more like a classic letter. I'm not sure how I feel about the content though.

**To: Penelope Williams**
**From: Rebecca Whitney [Spent]**

**(via Google Offworld Exchange)**
Hello Penelope,

It was good to hear from you last week. I am glad your training is going well. I remember what preparing for Academy exams feels like and I do not envy you compressing three years of work into one. If any Witch can do it, you can. You have lots of power, yes, but you also have personal strength. Sometimes I wonder if that might be more valuable.

I did have some news that I felt you needed to know. I wasn't sure how to tell you or if you wanted to know at all. Especially with how you saw them last. Your parents have divorced at last. Your mother took a new house not too far from town and your father moved away with your brother. I doubt either of them will return. Your mother works for her church now as their secretary and seems to be settling in well. Your old house was sold to a nice couple who moved from Brunswick.

I know you would rather let go of them, and I think it is wise to do so. I know you are still angry at them and still hate them. Your feelings are valid and what they did to you, especially your father, warrants that reaction. Eventually the rage will catch up to you. I hope you find closure for yourself, not for anyone else. It will set you free of the pain of your past.

I hope to see you soon. Keep your head on straight. Trust the ones you trust the most. Especially that one. And

don't be afraid to break the rules once
in a while. It will do you some good.
Your friend in power,
R. Whitney

The letters course through me. I can't help reflecting on what Lucy and Rebecca Whitney wrote. What I feel and what happened not even a year ago. I rub my left wrist, feeling the phantom of pain there and touch my lip trying to put it behind me.

Can I let go of that pain? Of that history?

I'm not sure I can.

7

## *BEFORE*

My room is dark. The lightbulb went out in my lamp a week ago and no one has bothered to replace it. It doesn't matter. I am behind my bed, up against the wall, curled up trying to make myself as small as possible.

Downstairs they are yelling.

"I don't care! I'm not taking her with me!" my father shouts.

"I don't want her with me either!" my mother yells back.

Some indistinct words before I hear something hit the floor and break. I don't think it was thrown, not from what it sounds like.

"She's your fault. You deal with her."

The last was my father.

Heavy footsteps ascend the stairs. I hug my knees knowing I can't do anything. Even teleporting is not possible right now. I barely remember the complicated spell matrix Altair taught me last week. Anything I write down gets thrown out.

The lock clicks.

My father comes barging into the room. I flinch at the anger in his face and recoil from him. He marches over to me and grabs my wrist in a way that makes Ikthiel's claws feel gentle.

I pull back from the contact and he says, "Stop it. You're coming with me."

My feet drag across the carpet. I manage to get my legs under me in time for the stairs, but I trip several times on the way down, my arm held up almost above my head. I am so small and my father seems enormous in his rage.

Stumbling down the stairs behind my father, I see my mother at the base. Her eyes widen when she sees me and how my father grips my arm. My brother is nowhere to be seen. I'm not even sure he is home, but it doesn't matter. He is no longer an ally.

The last step comes up abruptly. Instinctively I use my power to try and stop myself from falling. But I cannot fly so I come down with a thud. My father drops my wrist.

"You're taking her with you."

"No."

"It's your fault. I don't want either of you around anymore."

Suddenly it clicks. My parents are divorcing. It's not shocking exactly, but I'm more stunned their religion isn't getting in the way.

"I don't want her with me either!"

They are talking over me as if I'm not even there. They're arguing over which one has to deal with taking me in. I'm nothing to them. I'm a piece of furniture to be argued over in divorce court.

I can't take it anymore. My anger gets the better of me.

"What is wrong with you?" I spit the words at my father.

WHAM.

I don't even see the hand before it claps across my cheek and sends me into the tile floor. My eyes focus on the dust motes under the counter. For a moment that's all I can focus on.

"Alex! You can't!" my mother interjects.

"See?" he says icily. "She's *your* daughter. You're still protecting her."

I push myself back up off the floor. My father rewards me with another smack.

"Stop!" my mother says. "You're leaving a mark!"

*That's* what she's worried about?! Protecting herself and him from anyone knowing?

At this point my face throbs from the hits. I turn to walk

away through the kitchen aiming for the back door. My father grabs my wrist again twisting it painfully.

"STOP IT."

This time the protest is mine.

"No one else could knock this witch nonsense out of you," he says with venom in his voice. "Maybe I should try."

The next blow hits the back of my head so hard it knocks me to the ground. My vision goes dark then clears a couple times. The whole room swims before my eyes.

I had taken some injuries in my training, but this is so much worse. Those were accidents. This is deliberate.

I don't even get off the floor before the next blow. My head swims so much it takes a moment to recognize he hit my left ribs. My mother is screaming I think. So is my father. I can feel my power seething inside of me, but I can't focus. I can't see what to do. My mind fogs over more with every blow.

The cool of the kitchen floor feels soothing to my cheek even as the pain radiates from everywhere else. The tears hitting it feel hot and cold at the same time. I try to focus on the dust motes under the cabinet again but every moment it gets harder. Every time I reach for my power it gets harder to see, to feel. To know I am a Witch and have that ability.

There is blood on the tile in front me, coming from my face.

I think to myself, *I don't want to die.*

Abruptly the blows stop.

Relief floods through me intertwined with the excruciating pain. I am curled into a protective ball on the floor. Even breathing sends knives of pain through my body.

"Penelope?" a voice says softly.

It takes a moment to recognize Ikthiel.

"I have Altair and Alicia with me."

Those names mean nothing for a moment while I try to collect the scattered pieces of my brain. Then I understand. Ikthiel came with them. Alicia Cole. An adult.

"You're safe now," he says softly. "You can drop the shield."

I squeeze my eyes shut trying to understand what he's saying. Trying to feel anything but pain and panic.

"Penny?" Altair's voice this time. "Harilsen's coming with a healer. Can you let me examine you?"

Quietly, I hear Altair murmur to Ikthiel, "She's not breathing well. I think her ribs might be broken."

My eyes are still squeezed shut when I whisper, "Ikthiel."

Finally the demon's claws are in my hand. I feel Altair behind my back gently probing my spine with his fingers. A sharp intake of breath sends tired alarm through me. At this point I can barely feel shock or fear, my nerves are so fried.

Altair's fingers disappear. "I'm telling Harilsen to hurry. There's swelling around her spine."

Ikthiel's claws squeeze mine and for a moment I can hear his thoughts. I can barely make them out in my tangled brain, but I hear the deep concern there. Something about my situation scares him badly.

When two more people appear in the room, I register it this time. Altair immediately moves out of the way. I grip Ikthiel's hand, not even minding the added discomfort of his claws. It is such a minor, normal feeling compared to everything else.

"She won't let go," he says, explaining to someone else.

The stranger says, "It's ok. I can work with it." To me, they say, "Penny? I'm Thiltran. I'm a healer. I'm going to examine your spine."

I feel something press into my back that forces me to cry out. My eyes fly open, my hand gripping Ikthiel with what little strength I have left. I can see Alicia Cole and Harilsen across the room, the latter practically standing over my father. My parents look disheveled, as if they had been knocked over and just gotten back up. Their backs are to the dining table, situated at the far end of the kitchen. Neither of them takes a seat. My mother leans out from behind Harilsen, surreptitiously watching me. For a second I make eye-contact with her and all I can see there is pity.

I close my eyes again.

The warmth of healing power feels instantly recognizable. Thiltran carries significant strength, thankfully. I am afraid I need it.

"She has three broken ribs. One vertebra has a thin fracture in it, and the surrounding tissue has been badly traumatized. I need to stabilize this before we move her," Thiltran says in a calm, clinical voice.

Ikthiel squeezes my hand and answers, "I will stay and give you power if you need it."

"Same," Altair says from somewhere behind me.

"Altair," Alicia Cole says softly. "Will you go to Penny's room and pack her belongings? You know where everything is?"

"Yes," he says. I hear him leave and his footsteps recede up the stairs.

Thiltran presses on my upper spine, down near my tailbone, and then a third spot near the injury. For the first time I realize Thiltran is not human and probably has tentacles. Ikthiel squeezes my hand and pushes into my mind what he's seeing. Thiltran most closely resembles a land-walking octopus, just with the ability to hold themself upright. The image disappears and I realize Ikthiel was careful not to look down at me.

The pain suddenly abates, distanced from my mind somehow and pushed away while Thiltran works. The feeling of his healing power lulls me into a trance of sorts, helping to keep me still. Some time later I see Altair in my field of vision, the small backpack in his hand containing the sum total of my belongings. Alicia Cole's eyes burn with white hot anger as she looks at me and looks at my parents. I miss what she says, but my father storms out of the room followed by Harilsen.

Alicia Cole says something to my mother. The only word I catch in response is "divorcing."

My mind comes back just long enough to hear Alicia Cole say matter-of-factly, "But Penny is not safe with you either."

"No," my mother admits, looking down at me where I lay on the floor. "Not for the same reasons."

Because she doesn't love me anymore.

Ikthiel wraps his other hand engulfing mine. Altair crouches in front of me, blocking me from my mother's view. He puts a hand on my forehead, gently soothing my sore face. He's only three years older than me. The sadness in his face makes me wonder.

In this moment, I don't have space to ask those kinds of questions or hear the answers. My heart feels filled with venom. The ring of two friends and a healer buffer me from the toxicity of my home.

I don't know how long I stay on that floor, feeling Thiltran work. Finally, they say, "I need to turn her over."

Thiltran's tentacles cradle my spine while Altair takes my head to keep from bumping it on the floor. Ikthiel still holds my hand and moves so I can roll onto my back. The spine is tender where Thiltran worked on it.

Looking up at the ceiling now, my gaze meets the eyes of the healer. From this angle their skin appears bluish, but it's likely just a trick of the light. Three or four tentacles probe my face so gently it doesn't hurt. Then a tiny bit of healing power comes out of the tip of each tentacle, sinking deep into the bruises and the breaks in my face.

Thiltran murmurs, "Left cheekbone fractured. Moderate concussion."

That must have happened when my face hit the floor. The concussion should alarm me, but I don't have much energy for that now. Every ounce of worry and pain is gone, replaced by numbness.

Thiltran stops healing and Altair and Ikthiel look at them expectantly.

"That's all for now," they say. "I will stay on the planet tonight and examine her again in the morning."

"I've made arrangements for us tonight," Alicia Cole says. She glances around at the humans, aliens, and demon in my parent's kitchen. "You all need to make sure you look human to anyone who sees you."

"Teleport?" Thiltran asks.

"Yes, will that be safe?" Alicia Cole replies.

Thiltran considers for a moment. "Someone will need to carry her, but it should be safe enough."

"I'll carry her," Ikthiel volunteers.

Around me, everyone shifts their positions. Alicia Cole

speaks to Altair for a moment. Thiltran steps back to give space. Ikthiel moves to my side and puts an arm under my shoulders. His other arm he scoops under my knees and then lifts me like I weigh nothing. I'm not sure I don't weigh nothing to him.

A glance at the kitchen floor tells me how much blood must have come from my nose and mouth. I quickly look away from the red-brown stain. I rest my head on Ikthiel's shoulder and glance for a moment across the room. My mother still stands there, seemingly frozen in place. Her eyes watch me as I am carried by a demon. Altair remains between me and my mother, a casually protective position I didn't expect out of him. Harilsen comes back into the room now, my father trailing behind looking cowed.

"It's time?" Harilsen asks.

"Yes," Alicia Cole answers, picking up the bag Altair prepared. She and Harilson join the rest of us in the kitchen.

One by one, hand and tentacle find their way to Altair's shoulders and Altair puts his hands on Ikthiel and me.

For just one second I let myself look at my parents across the room. The parents who so blatantly rejected who I am that they couldn't love me in spite of it. My father's face is blank as the wall beside him, a frozen statue of disdain and suppressed rage. *Good riddance*, he is thinking.

My mother's features project a mixture of anger, fear, and regret. She doesn't know what to think anymore. Her whole world is collapsing around her and she is left to pick up the pieces. Still I can feel her mentally and emotionally distancing herself from the fact that I am leaving. I can feel her shutting down every motherly instinct to keep me from going.

In that moment the kitchen disappears around us.

We reappear at the dark end of a parking lot, hidden in the shadows. A building with a Days Inn sign looms in the distance. We are on the outskirts of town.

Silently I acknowledge that I may never see my parents again. A part of me breaks as I realize they prefer it that way.

I sink deep down into myself, letting the numbness and pain take over. I don't care anymore.

At least that is what I tell myself.

8



A tremor in the ground of Kaldreesa wakes me up in the middle of the night. I hold still for a moment listening to the various sounds of breathing in the room. The Kaldrasticans' deep breaths sound a bit like ocean waves back home. I sleep on the dais with Imfra-Rega's two youngest children and Altair, who is asleep across from me. My body feels stiff from sleeping on the hard surface, but they did give me a soft pillow, so at least my neck doesn't hurt.

I feel the tremor again and this time I move. I turn my head around and look over my pillow behind me to where Altair is sleeping, his head toward me and his body radiating away from me. On either side of me, the bulk of the Kaldrastican children form a protective flank.

Altair is deeply asleep. I sit up in the dark and see only stillness across the home in the recessed area where Imfra-Rega and her life-mate sleep. No one stirs for an earthquake on Kaldreesa except for those who have not lived here long.

I wait a moment before climbing to my feet. I wrap my blanket around me and walk on silent bare feet across the house. My gaze goes out into the deep darkness that is Kaldreesa at night. The earth is calm below my feet. Tentatively, I place one foot on the dense gravel of the plateau.

As I walk across the expanse of dark stone and tiny rocks, I marvel at how my feet are accustomed to the pressure after only a week here. At the end of the plateau, I pause and look out over the valley. The dark is somehow soothing. Maybe it is only that the darkness has no expectations of me.

The soft breeze touches my skin as I wait for the next tremor if it will come. I breathe and stand sure-footedly at the edge of a lethally high cliff with an air of confidence I didn't have six months ago. Time wanes onward, the turning of the sky a swathe of stars and galaxy and moon and color and night. The view is bigger than all of me, bigger than the smoldering fire eating away at my core. A longing surfaces deep inside: the desire to stay, watching that view for the rest of my life.

At some point my soul settles. I turn away from the cliff's edge and walk back to the dwelling.

No one has stirred from the time I woke to when I get back. I lay back down in the stillness of the home, all the Kaldrasticans and Altair sleeping on around me.

I don't know how long until I fall asleep. Before I realize it, morning is upon us.

I am the last one on the dais. The children have left for their version of school (which does not resemble school how I know it to be). There is peace in the home at this hour.

My morning routine on this world remains largely the same as back on Widdershin and on Earth. No one disturbs me while I wash and dress and find something to eat in the corner of the food storage crate where Imfra-Rega has carefully set aside food we can digest. It is only when I am sitting at the edge of the home, my bare feet resting lightly on the gravel ground, that Altair comes to sit next to me. I set the last pickings of my breakfast aside and wait.

"We'll be going back to Widdershin tomorrow."

I know this already. There is something else Altair is going to tell me. So I don't say anything. Impatiently I wait.

Altair takes out his own pseudo-smartphone and scrolls through to a particular message. He hands it to me saying, "I wasn't supposed to show this to you, but you should know what's going on in out there."

I look at him incredulously. Altair never seemed like the person to break the rules. He seemed straightlaced to me. But then I realize I don't know him at all. I don't know him on a personal level. I don't know him well enough to say whether he would break the rules or not.

The message reads as follows:

> **Location:** Marquis Delta Belt
> Reetur Family advancing.
> Outpost outnumbered.
> Influence gaining. Send Liaison.
> - MM

I read it twice trying to understand the odd message. Finally I just turn to Altair and ask, "What does it mean?" I hand him back is device.

Altair explains, "The Reetur family are Witches who believe we should all renounce our sparkpoints. They feel the constraints we put on ourselves is a violation of free will."

The description is familiar. The idea that the Witch's Spark, the power within each Witch, has a single purpose which sets the Spark into a blaze: that is the sole reason Witch's practice. They believe that even if the sparkpoint causes their death, they are doing their duty, that there is some need. In some ways the belief is closely related to religion. And the way Spent Witches speak of their sparkpoints, the moments when their power ignites to its full strength, those descriptions sometimes make me pause and wonder.

"Who is MM?"

Altair smiles wryly. "I only just learned her name: Madge Matxino. She is our contact in the region and she seems to have a personal vendetta against the Reeturs," he explains. "She is a formidable Witch, still before her sparkpoint. She feeds information to Widdershin through me. Everything she passes is classified. It's specifically barred from your knowledge."

"Why?" I ask, unable to see the need for that specificity. I don't often get indignant, but this is an odd restriction.

The expression on Altair's face is inscrutable. "They believe you could easily become a demon," he states bluntly.

I grind my teeth. Most days I feel anger at something in my life, whether it is an old demon from my past or some new irritation that crosses the line. This provokes the fury I keep pushed down below the surface. Altair seems to know what I am feeling because he leans back slightly. I don't say anything I just feel the fury burning through me.

It's the same thoughts my parents have: my power is of the devil, my power is evil. Does no one have respect for me? Does no one have faith in me? They all think I am corruptible. What about *my* choices?

I breathe through the anger and finally say one word through gritted teeth, "*Why?*"

Altair's answer is equally clipped, "Your anger."

I roll my eyes and turn my head away. Anger is my refuge most days. Anger keeps me from hatred, from cold brooding malevolence. Even Ikthiel worries I might succumb to hatred eventually.

"What is happening in the Marquis galaxy?"

"The Reeturs are gaining influence there," Altair says simply. I don't understand the significance, but never having been explained the full workings of the Witch community does make it difficult to make sense of basic politics.

I don't ask. Alicia Cole made it plain long ago that I would be told what I needed to know, that my power didn't grant me special access to normally classified information. Come to think of it the only Witch who was ever fully honest with me was Mrs. Whitney, all that time ago back on Earth.

Altair looks out across the open plateau. I wonder what he is looking at when I realize this is actually his home and he is just watching the landscape. Not for the first time the question comes to me: Why is Altair in our universe and not his own?

This time I finally ask.

The surprise on his face when he looks at me is significant. My reputation includes the fact that I do not want to know personal details. Out here Altair is as close to a friend as I can get. And I don't have friends here. My only friend is still back on Earth.

Altair considers for a moment, perhaps gauging if I am sincere. I don't know what he sees in me in that moment, but he must trust me with it because he begins to tell me his story.

And I sit in stunned silence, listening to the truth unfold.

"I was born on Earth. Not your Earth, *my* Earth," he begins. "My world, my home, was very different from what you know. Our universes are similar but different in ways I have not completely managed to define. But in the ways that you understand, it is the same. Gravity, time, light—they are all the same but slightly different.

"My Earth was the fifth planet around an old star. I was young when I left it last, so I do not remember much. But I remember my parent's faces. And I remember my house. Earth was a rocky planet, not so much water as yours, not so much green, but much bigger. I cannot prove this, but I do not think my Earth could exist in this universe. I think gravity is just different enough that it would not hold together here."

He pauses and swallows hard before going on.

"As you probably guessed my power came out when I was very young. I was probably an infant when my parents first saw the signs of it," he continued. I could see how much it cost him to speak about his parents. "They were Witches too, though we're not called that there. My parents had power, the kind that never seems to find its limits. Like yours in some ways."

The smile Altair gives me is the most genuine I have seen in a long time. From anyone, come to think of it.

A shadow passes across his face.

"Unlike here, our power is not concentrated in a single event. We can control the ebb and flow, and I have retained that somewhat since coming here," he explains. "We can choose when to use more or less of it. My parents were gifted like so many others, the same simple ability. They could give their power away."

The thought surprised me, though I don't know why it would or should. Surely Witches could share their powers, and it was obvious Altair did. He often gave Ikthiel a fraction of it.

"We were caught unaware," he says. "In the age we lived in, with the technology and the strengths we had, I think we became complacent that we would be prepared for anything. I don't know, because I was just a child. But I think my parents knew.

"For as long as I could remember they showed me pictures of our sister planet Wethtar in our neighboring system, some thirteen light-years away. The first human colony was there and it became a second homeworld after a while. When I was five years old, I found out why they drilled me on that planet." Altair eyes focus on the ground. For a moment he is silent.

"We didn't know until it was too late. We didn't see what was happening until there was no time to save anyone," he says, nearly choking on the words. "I don't know what it was. There are many hypotheses of what caused it, but it wasn't an object, so it's difficult to know for sure. Either way, everything in the system was obliterated. All the planets and moons gone. The sun shuddered and barely held on."

A pause and then he says, "My parents gave me every ounce of power they had. Everything. I think now that my mother must have seen the future and she never told anyone she could do that." He closes his eyes. "They told me to go. To take myself to Wethtar. I remember the sound of my mother's voice telling me to picture it and take myself there. I remember crying and begging her not to make me go. I remember my father telling me to leave, to live on."

The words are causing him pain to speak. I know pain, but this pain I have never felt. This is grief and guilt. He doesn't believe he should have survived while his entire planet burned. He thinks he should be dead right now.

I cannot find any words to say. So I sit in silence and watch him.

"I landed on Wethtar safely. All my homeworld were dead. I lived, as my father wanted," he says bitterly. He pauses and I think he is done, but he adds, "I was eleven when I figured out I could jump to other universes. And it was around that time that I realized I kept the power my parents gave me. It's mine now, but the price was very high."

He shakes his head and looks at the landscape of Kaldreesa. "In the past five years I have returned to my home universe only three times. This is not the only one I reside in, but I think this has become my home for now."

This is where he ends his story. The horrifying tale of unexpected death from space sends a feeling of cold through my body. For a fraction of a second I think about the Edge and then the stray thought disappears as quickly as it comes. One question enters my mind and I have to ask him.

"Why Kaldreesa? Why Imfra-Rega?"

Amusement flickers through his face. "You of all people should understand." He studies me and waits.

"I don't. I like them, but I assume you picked them before you met them? Isn't that how it usually works?"

Altair nods. "Yes, I did pick them. Kaldrasticans are distinctly different from humans," he says. "I know you isolate yourself on purpose. I didn't want a human family to live with here."

I look out at the orange landscape and feel deep down that despite my attempts to hide myself Altair has completely understood me. My family treated me with contempt. I would not wish to replace them. Altair chose Imfra-Rega's family for the opposite reason.

"Are we friends, Altair?"

"I think of you as a friend, though I don't think you want any," he answers.

I swallow. "I don't really. I have one friend back on Earth." I look at him and add, "But I think what you just told me makes us friends."

He looks amused again. "I considered you a friend after I found out you couldn't fly."

I roll my eyes. He is referring to the time years ago when I hit the ground when trying to fly. I got the hang of it later, but by far it was the skill that took me the longest to learn.

"You're just one of us," he says. "Everyone's scared of you, but most people aren't good judges of character. Ikthiel likes you. Imfra-Rega likes you. And I like you. Despite your horrible attitude most of the time."

I look at him levelly. "I doubt my attitude will improve," I say. "And isn't it odd for a Witch to trust a demon before other Witches?"

"How do you know Witches aren't demons in my universe?" he asks. "And how do you know you aren't a demon already?"

The questions catch me by surprise. I could ask him about the first one, but I know the second one will plague me for a long time. Instead of answering I just continue to stare out at the landscape in silence. Altair stays with me for a while and then leaves to go get his things gathered for the return to Widdershin.

Even as I am saying goodbye to Imfra-Rega later, feeling the warmth of her farewell, I am thinking about that conversation and his last questions to me. I had been taught Witches could sense the difference between other Witches and demons. It just never occurred to me that Ikthiel's power felt no different than Altair's or Harilsen's or even Alicia Cole's. So just what is it that makes a demon a demon? Is it really the power or is it something else?

I find myself thinking about this even as I take Altair's hand to leave Kaldreesa. As Widdershin manifests around us, the transport quad bustling with activity at the end of break, I watch Witch after Witch pass us and silently wonder how many of them could be demons after all. And whether I really am different from a demon or if that is what scares the other Witches.

.

9

*BEFORE*

"My family hates me," I whisper to Ikthiel who sits hunched in a dark corner of my bedroom. He's been here so much in the three years since I met him that he is not just comfortable, he's practically a piece of furniture.

"They do," Ikthiel answers in his blunt, tactless way.

I am almost thirteen years old. Three years ago this would have upset me more than it does now. In the years that have passed since then, I have heard it frequently. I've even heard it in their thoughts. I feel it is true. It doesn't make it any easier to accept, but it does mean I'm no longer fighting with myself over it. I am a pariah in my own family.

We are sitting in my dark, sparsely-decorated bedroom, watching out the front windows and seeing my parents and brother pull away from the house together. I am left at home alone because, according to my father, I don't deserve to go to the Christmas festival. Ikthiel popped in a few minutes after my mother shut me in my bedroom. They have taken to doing this recently, convinced they can keep me confined with a locked door. Walls and doors have not confined me in years. Thanks in part to Ikthiel and Altair.

"We should go somewhere," Ikthiel says, startling me out of my thoughts. He says it as if he knows I'll agree. He's not wrong.

"Where?"

"When will they be back?"

I shrug. "I can leave an alarm on the driveway and the front door so we can come back when it goes off."

He looks intrigued. I haven't told him about that particular spell matrix. I worked it out a couple weeks ago and have tried it several times since then. The range on it is enormous. I could be halfway across the solar system and still hear it.

From what I understand, most Witches used props of some kind to help them hold their matrices steady. Some use a book or a computer or some other tangible item. I don't have that luxury.

My room is spartan in design. My parents removed most frivolous objects. Even the teddy bear I had since I was a baby was taken away. They took the advice of the Jesus camp they sent me to last summer. The whole room reminds me of that oppressive environment. I came back from the summer and found everything I owned with the exception of my clothes had been thrown out. Everything. Five months later and I'm still feeling the sting of that loss. Some things you can never replace.

Now I try to memorize everything. Every nook and cranny of every room I visit in space. I can't take pictures, they might be thrown away. My parents fundamentally disagree with the nature of a large, old universe. I used to have a moon rock from my first trip up there when I was eleven. Even that is gone. So I simply keep my memories now. I cram as much into my head as I can. I hold onto it to remember.

The matrix is easy to hold in my head. I kept it simple to make it as infallible as possible. It's nothing more than a closed ring, designed to break if anyone human enters the house. I learned the hard way to structure it that way.

I form the matrix with my hands and my mind. My hands are cupped before me. Ikthiel watches with interest from across the room. I draw the circle within my mind's eye and it forms over my hands. A red line pulsing in a loop. It is bright in my dim room, but it will be invisible when I let it go.

The time it takes to structure it never passes quickly. I usually don't realize it is over. I just let the ring go and it expands and reforms around the house. If a dog or a cat or a squirrel passes into the ring, it won't call me back. But if a human comes to the front door or enters the house, I'll know right away and can get home.

"Skillfully done," Ikthiel remarks. It's a high compliment from him.

I take a deep breath and look around my sparse room. My bed is made neatly. My nightstand is bare except for the lamp, my only light. In the corner I have a tiny table and chair to function as a desk. My school things form a tidy stack in one corner, the few pens and pencils and other supplies given to me to prevent my parents from being suspected of child abuse. My clothes are neatly in my closet, all conservative dresses, skirts, blouses, and sweaters. I'm wearing a conservative dress with a cardigan right now. Sometimes I feel ridiculous.

"Where are we going?" I ask Ikthiel.

"Have you been to Mars?" he asks.

I look at him and try to gauge if he's being nice. His face is impassive. He might be trying to be nice. "No," I say. "But it is difficult for me to breathe there."

Ikthiel gives me a crooked smile. He opens his closed fist, his claws revealing a small piece of technology. It is about the size of a quarter and about five times as thick. He turns it over and unfolds two flexible lengths.

"Hold out your wrist," he says.

Obediently I hold out my right arm. He wraps the band around my wrist, a beetle-shaped piece left on top. I tightens significantly. I wince slightly and Ikthiel glances at me. Again I am reminded not to show a demon any weakness.

"It's a portable atmosphere," he explains. "It will last a few hours."

I nod, rubbing my wrist and looking at it.

"Let's go."

Ikthiel takes my arm and the world goes dark around us.

I feel the atmosphere kick in before my eyes register what I am looking at. A flush of cold rushes over me for a brief millisecond before the atmosphere warms me in the cold environment. I take a deep breath and let my eyes adjust to the light. It's dimmer than expected here and I'm blinking to understand it. The sun high above is bright but far away. A cold noontime sun.

Ahead of us is a massive shape emerging from the ground. Something tickles in my memory and I find myself remembering pictures of Uluru deep in the Australian outback. Except it's tanner. And incredibly massive. Like Uluru, it is remarkable and stunning.

I know the name of this place from an Earth Science class last year. Olympus Mons. When I look behind us to get my bearings, I realize we must be smack in the middle of Tharsis. Tharsis Montes recedes into the horizon behind us.

"Do you know what this is?" Ikthiel asks.

I nod. "I read about it last year."

The sheer size of it is overwhelming. I saw a graphic which overlaid the outline of Olympus Mons on the outline of France. France was bigger, but not by much. And Ikthiel has landed us far enough from it that it is easy to appreciate its overwhelming grandeur.

"Does anyone live here?" I ask. This is the question I wondered about since last year.

"No one now," Ikthiel answers. "It's a bit of a tourist hub though. They have to be careful about coming here now that Earth is watching so closely, but still. It's a geologically unique area and the volcano is impressive."

"Anything like this where you come from?"

Ikthiel looks at me in surprise. "Nothing like this," he says regretfully. "Though there are volcanoes on my homeworld. And mountains. Not much water though."

He gave me more detail than I expected. I wonder about him more than I wonder about Altair or Harilsen. I still know barely anything about him and we've known each other for three years.

"You never ask me anything," Ikthiel says, presumably in response to my thoughts.

"Oh," I say. "I'm out of practice." It's only half a joke. For the past three years, I've gotten more and more introverted. I don't like talking to people as much as I used to. I think I'm too afraid of being discovered to be comfortable asking questions.

"Wise," Ikthiel remarks, responding to my thoughts.

I don't know if it is wise. I ignore the remark.

At that moment my alarm on the house goes off in the back of my head. Ikthiel hears it like he hears most things in my mind. He nods at me, acknowledging my need to go home.

"You could just stay out," he says. "Show them they cannot control you."

Somehow those words of empowerment tempt me far more than the power of standing on Mars. I breathe for a few minutes, delaying my inevitable acquiescence and return home. The temptation is strong and not much more would be needed to make me give in.

Ikthiel takes my hand, his claws pressing into my skin but not breaking it. "I know you're not ready to leave Earth permanently. But when you are, I will help you."

His eyes tell me I can trust him. And for one moment I probe his demon mind. He holds still while I do so, lifting thought after thought from that tangled mess in his skull. I can see the dark bank of memories, an impenetrable host of thoughts even he cannot fully penetrate. I'm not concerned with that right now. His intentions, while not entirely pure, are at least for the sake of protecting me. He basks in my power, his main reason for associating with me.

"Take me home," is all I can say.

Mars fades away and my bedroom comes into view around me. Below I can hear the door opening and my father's heavy footsteps on the stairs. Ikthiel lets go of my hand. With one wave the alarms have disappeared from the house and I sit down in my desk chair. Out the window I can see my parent's car idling in the driveway and my mother and my brother's faces in the windows. I don't know why they're back so soon.

My father's footsteps give me a split second warning before the door flings open.

I flinch in response and glance around the room in panic.

Ikthiel is invisible, but I can just see him out of the corner of my eye.

My father is a tower of anger and irritation scarier than Ikthiel's demonic qualities ever have been. I used to think he loved me.

"Your mother insisted I leave you something to eat. We'll be out late," he says. He tosses something small on the bed and slams the door shut. The lock turns and his receding footsteps are followed by the closing of the front door. Below, I can see him getting in the car.

Even from this distance my Witch ears can make out their words.

"What was she doing?" my mother asks.

"Sitting at her desk," my father responds. "What does it matter? I left her food. She won't cause us trouble now."

"Good," my mother says.

"This is your fault, Anne," my father says. I can almost see his angry gaze falling on my mother. "You should have told me."

"*I didn't know*," my mother hisses.

My brother's gaze remains fixed out the window. I stand in my bedroom window watching the car as it backs from the drive. The light comes on behind me. In that moment as my dad shifts gears and turns the car away, my little brother's eyes turn up to my window.

My mother says, "Don't look at her."

My brother sneers at me and faces forward in the car. I know I've lost him.

"I hate her," I can hear him whisper. "Can't we get rid of her?"

The silence in the car speaks volumes. A rolling coil of dread settles in my stomach. For the first time in a long time, I am genuinely afraid of what my parents are contemplating doing.

Ikthiel's hand on my shoulder startles me out of my dark thoughts.

I look up at him.

"Contact Altair after I go. Now," he says. "Tell him to get Harilsen and tell them both what you just heard. They should know."

My skepticism must show on my face. So many times have the adults in my life failed me.

"Penelope," he says softly. He never uses my nickname. "You are a valued person. You are the most powerful Witch we've ever seen. They will take care of you."

His dark eyes are open and honest, an unusual and significant contrast to my family.

My family.

They do not value me.

There is a ringing in my ears. My thirteenth birthday is only a month away. I feel older. I feel ancient. I feel jaded.

For some weird reason the demon hugs me. It is the demon offering comfort. My world keeps crumbling over and over again.

"You're safe Penelope."

I nod into his chest, the oddly cadenced heartbeat ringing in my ears.

"I can stay for a little bit if you want," he says. I pull back from him. His face has an expression I can't quite read. Something between compassion and disdain. Though I'm not sure for whom he feels the disdain.

The light will only be on for a couple of hours. I look at the food my father left on the bed. It is a single granola bar. I pick it up and inspect the wrapper as if I haven't eaten plenty like it before. I usually buy food at the school cafeteria with money I steal using my power. At home I don't have the luxury. The one time I stole food from the kitchen I was locked in my room for three days. I don't risk trying to take it now. It's not worth it.

I sit down on the bed feeling dejected and alone. The granola bar is hardly a meal.

"Are you hungry?" Ikthiel asks.

I am always hungry these days. Especially over the holiday breaks like this. Most of the time I feel like my family is trying to starve me to death.

"I will return," Ikthiel says. Before I can blink he is gone.

About twenty minutes pass, though I'm not sure exactly how

long. There are no clocks in my room. My watch is long gone as well.

When Ikthiel reappears he is holding several bags of food that smell heavenly. He sits down on the bed across from me. From the first bag he produces several cartons of Chinese food and chopsticks, soy sauce and duck sauce and spicy mustard, and fortune cookies. The second bag contains Italian food. The third bag has pastries from what looks like a fancy French bakery. The different scents all mingle into one strange but intoxicating smell.

"Where should we start?" Ikthiel asks.

I grin at him and pick up the lasagna. "You should start with the lo mein."

Together we dive in to the meal he has procured. I don't know where he got the food. I could ask and he would be honest with me, but I am so hungry I just don't care. So I take my fork and my garlic bread and I chow down on Italian food from someplace called Carmine's. And I move on to the lo mein and then I pick up the pastry bag. A warm chocolate croissant is waiting inside with three of its friends.

I hand one to Ikthiel and take one for myself. We tap them as if we are clinking glasses and then I eat the delicious pastry my demon friend has brought me.

I feel safe and loved.

# INTERLUDE

Ikthiel waits on the barren surface of a cold, dark moon. His demon eyes survey the empty space above him and silently, impatiently, he waits. His colleagues always keep him waiting. Young as Penelope is, her observation about his colleagues is correct: they are not friends.

Demons do not always remember what it means to be friends.

Ahead of him, on the horizon to his left, the last remnants of the ancient starlight dips below the horizon. This distant moon of this distant planet spins onward into the frozen dark. And against the blaze of old starlight peppering the sky, against the backdrop of stars and night, one by one the others appear.

Instinctively, Ikthiel tenses at their arrival. The five have him surrounded. He is strong, but certainly not strong enough to take on five demons at once. His only consolation is the familiar buzz of armor running over his body. Fashioned of Witch's armor and modified to adapt to his unique power, he feels protected even surrounded as he is.

"Ikthiel," the primary says. She is harsh in her appearance, always the demon. Ikthiel is half her age and maybe even less than that. She never reveals an iota of her true self if she can help it. She is the leader here, Romora of the Dryven's Sphere.

He does no more than nod in her direction as she approaches him. The four demons scattered around him maintain their distance, but he feels their power flex in his direction lest he attempt something on their leader. The smallest one to his right, the spritely female-esce Waspira, is by far the most dangerous. All the lessons of size and power are reinforced in Miss Williams: size has nothing to do with it.

"You have what we asked of you," she says. It is not a question. It is an order.

Ikthiel purses his lips. This is the answer he hesitates to give. "No," he says. "She has not given up her power yet."

Romora makes no move in his direction, an inaction that takes real restraint. He can feel the tides within her shuddering as she struggles to restrain herself. To his right he can feel Waspira tense and behind him Gethryl and Matchen shift uncomfortably. Only Disperao to his left makes no reaction. Disperao is not prone to sudden reactions: he is a space-time demon.

"She will not need to," Ikthiel dares to continue.

Silence meets Ikthiel's words. Romora is seething with anger at this point. Ikthiel is calm only because he has already seen his near future: a moment conversing with Penelope in only a day or so..

Before the angry demon's self-control slips and Ikthiel is faced with defending himself, he continues as calmly as possible, "The Witch girl can give up more than what we need and still be untouched. And she will do so willingly," he added.

"Why not just kill her and take all her power?" Gethryl says behind him.

Ikthiel makes no move and does not react. He simply says, "She is a living power source. Even if we managed to extract the power we need before killing her, she is much more valuable alive."

A memory of a vision, a future still a long ways off, flickers through his mind as he thinks this. The vision is incomplete and not nearly as detailed as he usually sees, but Ikthiel knows the importance from even just that one snippet. A cold shiver runs down his spine as he pushes the vision aside once again.

The demons around him are silent. He can feel the current of their minds as they decide what to do. Though Romora is the leader here, she lacks the perceptions the others have, especially Disperao. Where Ikthiel is a predictor demon and can catch visions of the future, Disperao's perceptions give him awareness and mastery of time itself. His kind are rare, but they are some of the most terrifying types of demons out there. Most Witches are unaware of their existence. But that is what they do: they wipe out existences from time. As easily as Ikthiel can see the future unfolding, Disperao can twist time so that his victim never existed. For this reason most Witches remain unaware of their power. The Witches who find out are often eliminated by time twists.

"You have one more chance," Romora says. "Do not come back again empty-handed."

She does not need to finish the threat. Ikthiel knows well what each of the demons around him can do.

Romora disappears without another word. One by one the demons each leave, Disperao the last to go.

An unsettled feeling comes over Ikthiel as he thought of their words and his assurances that he would get Penelope's power. She would need to give it up willingly for it to be useful to them. Her power would be corrupted if it was forcibly taken.

He looks up at the dark emptiness, no clues coming forth in the darkness. The unsettled feeling spreads as he contemplates the sky above and the most troubling reality of all: the uncertainty of human free will.

# PART 2

10

*NOW*

Time got away from me as I fell back into the routine of the Academy. My courses—what few of them I take—culminate to conclusion only when you have mastered the material they offer. I finished them one month after I returned from Kaldreesa. I moved on into courses akin to early college work back on Earth. The transition absorbed what little free time I had. I was forced to take a break from commission work for the time being.

All of this kept me from being able to think about my encounter at the Edge. Ikthiel remained banned from the Academy, so our meetings—rare as they were before—suddenly dropped off to nothing. My view of the Edge, the creatures I saw out there, worried me when I had a moment to think about it. I usually didn't have the time.

Then the first day of winter arrived.

Widdershin's winters are harsher than Earth's. The planet's tilt is such that it gets more brutally cold farther south than it ever would on Earth. I was told upon arrival that I would be completely unprepared for the difference. Today is a day like that.

I found myself sitting in the quad bundled up from head to toe, determined not to let the cold weather drive me indoors. I watch the people coming and going through the portals. Many of them move quickly, but some creatures I would expect to avoid the cold do not move with the same swiftness. It seems not all reptiles are averse to frigid temperatures.

"Penelope Williams?"

My name jolts me. I rarely hear it in full anymore. The voice calling my name belongs to a tall, scaled alien of a variety I have never seen.

The alien's features stun me with a kind of unexpected elegance that is arresting in its alien nature. Their body is vaguely humanoid, but it is as if their species evolved into it reluctantly. Long arms support stunted fins along their length and a long tail fringed with fins balances barely off the ground behind them. More fishlike than reptilian, this being moves likes they should be in water. As they come closer, I notice the personal atmosphere, probably a personal ocean, clinging to their skin. A fish as I understand them, but as they draws closer I see they are not scales after all. The muddy skin is not immediately attractive, but the changing sunset light gives away the iridescence I can imagine must be useful in their home ocean. The eyes studying me remind me of a whale's somehow, with the softness and pensiveness I associate with them. The face holding those eyes is elongated but vaguely human, a thought that surprises me as I realize it is true. I wonder what place they could be from and the kind of person they are.

"Hello," I say. It is the first pleasant word out of my mouth in weeks.

The hand she extends to me is equipped with seven atrociously long fingers each bridged by a web. I take the hand gently, fearful of hurting the delicate fingers, but I am immediately startled to find it strong.

"I am Firrl," she says to me. Her voice is feminine, and indeed her body could be described that way too. I hesitate to thrust my human notions of gender on such varying species and accidentally offending them. Firrl, however, seems female. I am almost completely certain of it.

"What can I do for you?" I ask, standing to greet her properly. Her height overwhelms me. It is a safe guess to say she is twice my height.

She smiles at me. "I've been asked to bring you to the research lab I work in," she explains. "I think you received the communication about it yesterday?"

I nod, acknowledging I remember. A group conducting millennia-long research has been tracking the occurrences of Witch's abilities and tracing their sparkpoints. As I am an unusual case, I was asked to come in and provide genetics, power samples, personal anecdotes, and whatever else they need to help with their research. I am no longer shy about giving those details away. The past few years and my short time at the Academy taught me not to care what others think of me. Too many would dislike me right away because of my power anyway. Eventually I just became numb to their reactions.

"Yes," I say. "I didn't realize it was almost time."

I get up off my usual wall and walk with Firrl a good three hundred yards to the nearest building. Inside I pull back my hood and take off my hat, gloves, scarf, and goggles. For just a second I see Firrl have the same reaction to me as I had to her. It's almost recognition, but not quite. Like we might have met before, but we're both sure we haven't.

Instead of commenting, Firrl leads me around the corner and down a long white hallway toward the other end of the building. Though this building houses mainly learning rooms, studies for the students, and various laboratories, the far end also houses a station for the Planetary Tram System, usually just called "the tram." The whole setup reminds me of monorail systems back on Earth, working on frictionless tracks and hubs and whatnot, but it's advanced in the extreme. We are crossing a distance the size of North America, but the trip will only take us about twenty-five minutes to complete.

Firrl and I are waiting on the platform for only five minutes before the next tram enters. We politely wait as passengers disembark, and a few minutes later I'm watching the frigid landscape fall away as we head south on Widdershin.

The landscape disappears almost too fast to witness, but the distant slopes of the Frontormin mountain chain stay in my view long enough to be appreciated. Firrl and I are both watching out the west-facing window of the tram, with our backs turned to the other passengers. I can feel eyes on my back, my reputation following me wherever I go. I doubt my face is recognizable. One Witch's power can recognize another, and each can discern the relative power levels. Not one Witch on the tram could ignore the feel of my power. We cannot ever hide from one another.

Fifteen minutes into the journey and the tramway turns to ride along the coast of the Great Bay of Tethys. Firrl stands significantly taller than me, even with her long tail coiled elegantly behind her. Her back fins she uses like stubby legs on land. As we circle the expansive bay, her body language changes and I wonder, for the first time, if she is missing home.

"How long has it been since you've been home?" I whisper.

She turns to me, surprise registering on her face, and she leans down to whisper back. "Two years," she says.

"Do you not get into the water very often?" I ask.

Her face is kind when she smiles at me sadly. "Our type of planet is rare," she says. "We have only ten percent surface area covered in land. It is disappointing to realize that your world is not normal."

Years of silence ingrained in me by my family holds me back. But then I say, "Earth is seventy percent water," remembering some figure I learned in school.

"Seventy percent?" she asks. Nostalgia fills her eyes. "My people would like it there."

I nod at her and, with only a moment's hesitation, I add, "My home was along the coast. Right up against the ocean."

"How far is your home?"

Bitterness seeps into me like oil in water. It must show in my face. Earth is not very far as Witch's travel. However, Earth is further than the Edge in some ways.

But all I say is, "Far."

My abrupt answer effectively ends the conversation, but Firrl does not seem to mind. We both go back to watching Tethys pass the tram window. In a moment the living memory is gone around the next bend of the tramway and our view fills with ambiguous mountains again.

The landscape gives way to a more tropical feel as we progress further south. By the time the tram arrives at our destination, the tundra has receded, giving way to the usual yellow foliage. Firrl and I disembark with a few other passengers before the tram speeds away to its next destination even further south.

"This way," she says softly.

I follow her through this station, past another conglomeration of labs and libraries and who-knew-what-else, to the far end of the building. I step outside in the open air for the first time in half an hour and I feel—*warmth*. Winter is so harsh on Widdershin that it chases away all remembrance of being warm. I open my jacket and let the warm breeze remind me of home.

Firrl is smiling at me and laughing with her eyes as I stand there and enjoy the weather for the first time in over a month.

"Is Earth warm?" she asks.

"Where I am from on Earth is almost always warm," I answer. "It gets cold there, but never like here. Never as cold as this place." And that, I realize, is true.

She is kind when she asks politely, "Are you ready?"

I take a deep breath and smile at her. "Yes, I'm ready now."

We begin to walk across the platform and away from the station.

The walk to the laboratory is a good half mile down from the station. The weather is such a change of pace that I find myself looking around at the scenery in deep appreciation for the first time in over a month. Widdershin owes its drastic shift in seasons to its deep axial tilt: $30.25°$ compared to Earth's more modest $23.5°$. My home region here is below the arctic circle, but the days are so short this time of year it makes it difficult to believe in spring. All around me, here nearer to the equator and close to the tropics, I am reminded of the home I left behind and nearly-everlasting warmth there.

*Here*, Firrl's voice reverberates in my head.

I whip my head around at her and look at the place in her mind. Her thought-voice is not so much words as it is concepts coupled with images.

"I apologize," she says. "I sometimes forget non-telepaths struggle to understand telepathy."

I shake my head, some bubbly feeling of delight growing in me. "Don't apologize," I answer. "I understood perfectly." I pause for half a second, but then plunge forward. "Do you think you could teach me that?"

Firrl is skeptical as we approach the main entrance of the building. I should mention that most doors on Widdershin are nearly fifteen feet tall and roughly four feet wide to accommodate the diverse species. Though Firrl is probably two or three feet taller than me, she is tiny in the doorway. I feel dwarfed by her, though I feel pretty small on a regular basis around here. Aliens are tall.

"I'm not sure it can be taught," she says as we cross into the shade inside the building. "Our telepathy comes from our physiology, not from our magic. My power is slanted toward foresight, like most of my species."

Again I feel a sense of deja vu. One of the facts about humans I learned at the Academy came as part of a general description of our species. Humanity, while brilliant in creativity and cunning, had the drawback of not tapping its highest potentials. Like with Firrl's species, foresight is a common gift among humans, though not the prevailing one. And human physiology does not preclude the possibility of telepathy, but the current theories on human evolution suggest the psychological component necessary to develop telepathy is not yet present. I think in some sense the authors of the studies questioned humanity's maturity, and struggled with any real reason why we hadn't developed it yet. Oddly enough, on a case-by-case basis, it is not unusual for a human independent of evolution to become a telepath.

Firrl's eyes are watching me and I realize she has been listening to my every thought. I stop in my tracks in the middle of the large vestibule we have walked into and I face her. I think at her very clearly, *Have we met before?*

Her expression flickers through several emotions rapidly. Then I hear her reply, *I wondered that as well.* I remind her of someone, but she cannot figure out who.

For a moment we just watch each other's expressions, but eventually when neither of us speaks or passes another thought, we head across the vestibule and toward a line of elevators. I take a glance around the vestibule while we wait for the elevator to come to us. The space resembles a fancy corporate building, but is void of a reception or a security station. Security is not exactly regarded lightly on Widdershin, but the whole planet is guarded by a defense net that only recognized Witches can teleport through. Individual security stations seem pointless. Beyond the lack of security, no foot traffic is present in the building. We are the only ones here.

*It is not a busy building,* Firrl remarks, catching my train of thought. *Specialized research buildings never are.*

I look at the walls made of heavy stone, a stone reminiscent of black granite or dark marble back home, and study the lights coming from recesses in the ceiling. The lights are not natural, but are not the usual sources I see all over Widdershin. They are dimmer for one, and seem to have a different source for another.

*The building is as old as the research itself,* Firrl explains. *They are the old-style power-based lights. We fuel them about once a year.*

Everywhere else on Widdershin uses the more "modern" light system which, to me, seems like a fancy, upgraded version of halogen bulbs. For a moment I think the power-based lights are more sophisticated.

*You're not wrong,* Firrl says. *My homeworld uses Guardian lights everywhere.*

And that I can believe, as electricity seems impractical underwater.

The elevator dings, an echoing sound in the quiet vestibule. Neither of us has spoken aloud since we entered the main doors.

I step into the spacious elevator with Firrl by my side. She pushes the button for Floor "-12." I had not realized we were going underground. We are both silent as the elevator begins to descend.

A few floors deeper into the ground and my mind wanders again to thoughts of the building itself. I wonder inwardly why the research facility had been built so deep into the ground.

*They have not taught you Widdershin's history yet,* she says. It is less of a question and more of a statement of fact.

*No,* I think back as clearly as I can.

In my mind and echoed outside, I hear Firrl's fluttery laughter. I'm not sure if she's laughing with her primitive vocal cords or her gills to be honest. But the peal of laughter I hear in my head is like a cacophony of bells: joy-filled and unfiltered.

*I can hear you just fine, now that I know what your inner-voice sounds like,* she explains. *You have no need to shout.*

I smile at her. The only sound in the elevator is the rhythmic swishing of the floors as they pass by. My ears pop a couple times as we get lower underground. In my mind she answers my question with a story. It is unlike anything I have ever experienced. Images fill my mind accompanied by her relating the narrative.

*When the Guardians come to Widdershin, the planet is desolate, barren. The Guardians come in response to a distress call, like so many other places. This is in the Ancient Times, the Time before Time.*

I have come to realize that time is not the same for all species, that the concept is not as simplistic as I once understood. But even here, in this story, I do not completely understand what she means.

Until she shows me an image that I will never forget.

*Widdershin's sun is an ancient star, dating to the time of the earliest stars. It is not the oldest by far, and it certainly is not the first, but it is here before many others. Widdershin itself is so old that stars have birthed and snuffed around it well within its lifetime.*

My mind is filled with the early images of Widdershin's galaxy. The stars are so close together that it takes my breath away. I am so nervous just watching the images in my head, so afraid that the stars will come too close together and touch and be destroyed.

*Sometimes they do.*

A flair bursts across my mind and through the intervening space between Widdershin's sun and its neighboring stars. Widdershin's sun escaped the event, but the planet was not so lucky. The time it took for such a flare to reach across space like that had to be enormous. No wonder the people living on Widdershin were able to call for help. They had to have seen their doom coming for years, if they had the capability.

*There are a few Guardians on Widdershin in that time. They see the burning sky coming.*

I wonder for a moment what "burning sky" means.

In my mind's eye I see a gamma ray flash. I'm not sure how I know it's a gamma ray burst, but I think it might have something to do with the way Firrl communicates.

*The sky burns and the land falls to ash. All that lives here dies in that instant. By the time the Guardians arrive, the people of Widdershin are dead. And the land is no longer living.*

I see the wasteland left behind, the shadows on the ground, the red rock. All that remains of Widdershin's earliest inhabitants is a few handfuls of dust. The desolation fills my mind.

*As the stars grow distant from each other, as the World becomes less harsh, Widdershin quiets and the galaxy becomes calm. The Guardians work to grow Widdershin anew. They burrow deep underground in those first eons, they hide underground to live safely.*

The depth of the laboratory suddenly makes sense to me. The safety of the cavern, of the rock, must seem like salvation on a world where a whole civilization died from the burning of the sky.

*Yes,* Firrl says in my mind. *Even as the land shifts and the oceans swell and change, the Guardians still keep to the underground. Here where it is always safer.*

The elevator dings dully and my mind is brought back to the world around me. For just a moment I feel as if everything around me had been holding its breath while I listened to the story of the dying world. I wonder if Widdershin itself felt pain at the demise of its inhabitants. I wonder if planets can feel pain.

*My people believe they do,* Firrl says simply.

And we step through the door of the elevator and begin to walk down a long corridor in the depths of Widdershin. I am slightly behind Firrl, following her. As she walks before me, her mind resting gently in the back of mine now, I wonder again why I feel like I know this person. Who she is and who she reminds me of, and if we have ever met.

Remarkable, I think, to find someone so familiar in a place so alien.

# 11



*NOW*

"Remember to breathe, Miss Williams."

I force myself to take breaths and continue to keep myself as calm as possible. I do not always do well standing in a claustrophobic space. The tank they have me in is very small indeed, built for species roughly my size. The diameter cannot be more than two feet across.

"You should feel the scanner now."

The intercom startles me every time it goes off. Through the clear container sides, Firrl's face is distorted. She is watching me as I struggle through the testing.

And on cue I feel the soul-burning touch of the meters scanning me. My power, my Witch's Spark, is being pulled and pushed at as the scan passes through me. My brain shuts out the part that feels pain and the rest of me, the psyche, struggles to keep from bearing the desperation, the distress caused by the beam.

*Are you alright?*

Firrl's voice cuts through my mind like a flame to gasoline.

My eyes meet hers. Tears are forming and trying to fall now. Pain rattles me, a feeling like my bones are trying to shatter to get away from the pain.

The uptake node above my head explodes.

Relief is immediate.

All around the chamber the researchers scramble to get me out of the container. I rest my hand on the container wall again. The barrier disappears.

As one, the five researchers recoil from me.

Their reaction scares me worse than the pain and the explosion. My eyes meet Firrl's and her thought-voice confirms what I fear. *Yes, that was you.*

I step off the platform and my legs collapse under me. I am mentally and physically exhausted from feeling the torturous sensation of my soul stretched and skewed by their test. I don't even understand how such a thing is possible. And my ignorance is making me crankier. No motivation strikes me to even attempt to hide my feelings for all this. They hover around me as I glare at them in contempt.

Over and over they tell me in stuttering tones that it's alright, that they have replacement parts, that they plan for this kind of thing, and on and on. Their words are hollow. Their reactions speak volumes. It is the kind of reactions to which I have had to become accustomed. My mental shields drop down in a moment of vulnerability. Maybe I am just too exhausted to fight back the tide. I am suddenly flooded with the range of emotional thoughts from each of the researchers.

I cannot fathom how a group of people can think both such kindnesses and such cruelties about me. These are the people who only moments ago reassured me that I did nothing wrong.

Firrl catches my eye.

Though there are no words, the tone of her thoughts is a tangle of worry for me. She is concerned that I might not be able to handle the swirl of thoughts around me. She is right, of course. I have not in the past allowed myself to hear the thoughts of others. I have chosen to remain deaf to their judgement, to their pain.

"I think we should stop for now," Firrl's voice rings out in the room. "It will take time to set the chamber up again, and we can continue later."

The group seems relieved by her suggestion. I know I am.

A few minutes of conversation later and I know when I need to report back to this part of Widdershin. I am resisting returning at this point, but I know it will help them and I am past the worst part of it. At least I hope I am past the worse part.

Once everything is settled Firrl offers to take me back to the surface. I say my goodbyes to the research group and feel their collective relief at my departure. I shrink a little inside at knowing I illicit such a reaction.

In the hall outside the research room, we walk a little distance away from the door before Firrl says anything. It is her inner voice I hear, though.

*It is hard for you, being the way you are.*

She says it so matter-of-factly that I think she understands. *No,* I think back at her. My heart just isn't in the conversation right now. It is nice that she doesn't ask me to speak.

Her many-fingered hand reaches over and squeezes my shoulder in support. I smile up at her. Again my smile feels out of place, but it is sincere this time.

*Will you ever return to Earth?* she asks suddenly.

I am surprised by the question, but in her mind I can see her picturing the endless ocean of her home and comparing it to the glimpses of the Atlantic she snatched from my mind. She probably knows that I don't believe I will ever return to Earth, but I choose to be kind for once.

*If I do, I will be sure to let you know.*

We are at the elevator by this point. We step inside and it begins to ascend back to the surface. Silence passes between us.

It's strange.

For the first time in months, I feel completely at home in someone's company. I close my eyes, letting the motion of the elevator soothe me. Slowly we rise to the surface.

12

***BEFORE***

Cold wood presses against my forehead. Frustration and anger run through me. I wonder what I must have done to deserve this. Could being myself be so *wrong?* How is this concept of sin so against those who didn't have a choice?

My forehead is slipping off the altar rail. I shift to correct my posture. Stiffness takes over my back. My legs have become fidgety in the past hour.

"WILLIAMS!"

I flinch at the sound of my name.

"I said be still!"

I clench my jaw in anger. The new power strains to be released at this very moment. All my willpower is required to hold it back. The demon taught me that the last time he saw me. He told me very clearly how bad it could be for me if I did not control my power. Deep breaths bring calm where simple desire is not enough.

I rest my head on the altar rail more firmly and brace myself for any further reproach. None comes. Ms. Minchion seems content to torture the next misbehaving student.

Secretly, silently, the hand of the girl kneeling uncomfortably next to me reaches over and pinches my pinkie. I peek out of my right eye and see Lucy St. John wink at me. How my best friend ended up at the same Jesus Camp I did, I'm not entirely sure. Her parents are not religious, but when I told her my parents made plans to send me here, she jumped on the bandwagon and said she'd come too. We've both been in trouble the whole summer, completely incapable of being serious as she is.

I am grateful in the month I have been here that all the girls share the same dorm. I am also grateful that all the girls are trouble-makers in the eyes of the program coordinators. Two of the girls hide contraband in false bottoms of their storage trunks and are not opposed to sharing chips, marshmallows, chocolate, white cheddar popcorn, rice crispy treats, and all the candy they could smuggle. Late after midnight I feel an odd solidarity with the girls here; all of us ages twelve to fourteen, all of us struggling with the religious oppression enforced by their families.

My whole life I have been around the religious. This world is so familiar to me in some ways that to find myself in a place like this where I am openly judged and mocked and rejected seems markedly foreign. On the whole, the church I grew up in never seemed extreme. I felt at home there and comfortable with my family. Then again, I was considered a part of the church, an insider then. Years have passed since I became the outsider.

In the hour that follows, my mind wanders back through the recent past. My family hates me. I know this more than believe this. I cannot understand it. Six more weeks stand between me and leaving this place. I feel trapped and hopeless sometimes. Most of the time wondering if other teenagers feel this way makes me feel isolated and alone. I'm sure they don't have the same struggle I'm going through.

Then again theirs could be worse.

We are released for the afternoon and we have an hour free before dinner. Lucy accompanies me on a walk around the campus. It's a small place, only four buildings and a chapel—the chapel we just came out of—surrounding a small quad with minimal landscaping and a statue of Jesus. We go and sit before the statue on one of the benches meant for praying, but instead we look fixedly at the statue while whispering to each other.

I finally ask the question that has been on my mind for weeks now. "Lucy, why did you come here?"

"I'm your friend, Penny," she says. She probably doesn't need to explain beyond that, but she continues anyway. "I don't know what has been happening between you and your family, but I thought you needed a friend this summer. When you told me you were coming here, I asked my parents to let me come along."

I glance at her out of the corner of my eye. "Why did they agree?"

"They could see the logic behind why I wanted to go," she says. Her mom is a biologist and her dad is a lawyer. Our families could not be more different. I think, in some sense, that is why we are such close friends. We have both attracted our opposites to ourselves.

"I didn't want to ask before," I admit finally. "I was afraid you would change your mind if I asked."

Out of the corner of my eye, I see Lucy smile. She doesn't say anything to me because at that moment Miss Minchion calls us back to our studies. She doesn't need to say anything else though.

I glance up at the statue as I rise and look over my shoulder at it as I walk away. I realize then that our pasts are all that we own in some sense. Lucy made a choice a couple months ago to be a better friend to me—better family—than my own family. That choice defined her present. My past, the past of my family and my lineage, defined who I am today. Intersections along our paths drew Lucy and I together.

As I come under the awning of the building, I glance over my shoulder one more time at the statue of Jesus. He seems to look at me, though it is probably my imagination. When I turn back from my thoughts, Lucy is watching me.

Just before we step into the building and return to the rigorous schedule of this place I whisper as softly as I can, "Thank you."

A tiny nod of the head is all Lucy is able to give in that moment. Her only acknowledgement of the pale words I can offer in return for her gesture.

# 13

*NOW*

I take back everything I ever said about the color orange. Silently, I gripe again about the foliage and the heat and the humidity on this God-forsaken planet.

Jungles on Earth are a tiptoe through the tulips compared to this place. Not that I have ever been to a jungle on Earth. I just cannot imagine them being as ridiculously brutal as this one. This whole planet is one giant jungle of death. Every ten seconds, I find myself dreaming of ice cream and lemonade and cool breezes and even the Arctic back home.

I am completely surrounded by dark, putrid green. Unlike the softened greens of jungles back home (at least the jungles I have seen in pictures), this green is unforgiving. The depths of its color borders on blue and black in some plants and reminds me of poisonous things.

The air here is breathable by my standards, but my personal atmosphere keeps kicking in to give me some relief from the humidity. More than a month ago Ikthiel told me he could teach me to breathe without the apparatus. I wish he already had. Moreover I wish he were here and I wasn't surrounded by strangers on this strange world.

This planet is small. It is roughly two-thirds the size of Mercury, which is to say it isn't much different than Earth's moon. As such, I have learned by this point that I shouldn't expect an atmosphere on a planet this size, much less overgrown vegetation, but the planet itself is massive enough to manage it. The gravity here is slightly heavier than Earth's, roughly 110%. The planet itself is composed of a higher percentage of heavy elements than Earth, though again the exterior structure is roughly the same. The atmosphere, as I have had to cope with, is much richer in water vapor lending to the heavier cloud cover seen from space. Down here it is apparent in both the tropical rainforest climate just about everywhere on the planet and the drowning humidity that has my hair clinging to my skull.

The ground rumbles below us.

"Again," a voice says behind me. One of the Witches in the crew is similar in species to a deer, if deer also had reptile skin. I glance back at him, his reddish eyes blinking at me in anxiety.

The ground trembles below us. Instinctively I reach out and lean on the nearest tree for support. The others ahead of me— with the exception of our native guide—all follow my lead and either reach for a support or outright sit down.

We are not in an ideal location to be experiencing the minor earthquake. Not only is this planet dominated by tropical rainforest but it is topographically mostly sharp hills and mountains. We are trekking through the rough foliage about three miles above sea level and will shortly be making our way down the other side of the volcano. However, until then, we have to endure the occasional tremor that seems keen on knocking us off our feet.

About ten or fifteen minutes pass and we are able to continue on the trail. I am in the middle of this mixed convoy, three ahead of me and three behind me. As usually I am here to provide a major power source to help quiet a volcano that has recently decided to endanger one of the largest cities here. Though the planet is small, there are still several million people who live here, mostly native ta-kef-ee like our guide. The Takeef are protective of their home. No matter the difficulty of living on a planet as volcanically active as their own, their attitude is that this is home.

Berkaan sits along the edge of the island Thell, just in the shadow of the volcano. Thell is an island in my human perceptions, but on a planet as small as Nahnu-beit, Thell is a continent. What little I learned of the geography before coming here reminds me again of how strange planets with oceans actually are. Most of my recent commissions have put me on planets with desert climates or temperate regions. Nahnu-beit is about half water, enough to fill the Atlantic ocean on Earth, no doubt a feature attributed to its ridiculous water content in its atmosphere. This is the only planet aside from Widdershin on which I have experienced rain since leaving Earth.

After a moment of each of us generally checking to make sure we hadn't broken anything, our guide leads us down the path along the backside of the volcano. Berkaan is down at the base on that side, but we hadn't been able to teleport right into the city. Even Altair wouldn't have been able to cut through the interference from the over-active volcano. He wasn't available for this trip anyway.

I feel as if the ta-kef-ee leading us thinks we are awkward by his species' standards. I watch him move with grace despite being a bird-reptile-something with claws and teeth and sharp binocular eyes and maybe many other things that make him formidable. His species flies and climbs and on occasion walks.

Besides the scaled-antelope (a species called the Dursan) and myself, we are a strange mesh of species that aren't exactly classifiable by human standards. Our heights and appearances vary greatly. Not one of us is well adapted to moving easily over constantly shifting ground.

We carefully navigate down the narrow path on the far side of the volcano. All is going well until we come to a particularly rough patch of land where the ground has eroded away from the trees. Our ta-kef-ee guide moves easily across the gap and guides the next one (a Granician who is made of fluid rock in varying shades of marble) across. I watch the Granician sprout extra legs and arms to help themself across. I wonder if earthquakes are this species' deepest nightmares.

After the Granician is another species of another strange

form: a blue-green Feirlu made of both plasma and matter. I'm afraid to accidentally touch their skin. However, the Feirlu is fairly graceful despite being fully subject to gravity *and* electromagnetic fields, so they slip across nimbly.

My turn.

I place a hand on the tree and grab hold of one of the exterior roots. The tree is a bit like a banyan tree back home, but the support roots are much thinner and woven together to form the overall structure. My fingers wrap tightly around it and I pay more attention to my footing. I take a step, transfer my weight—

*—and the ground gives way—*

The root snaps in my hand.

I lose track of what happens next. I feel hit after hit as I tumble down the side of the volcano and run into tree after tree (or rock?) and feel the bruises forming.

My head is jarred—

14

## *BEFORE*

I sit stiffly in the principal's office on the last day of seventh grade. My left arm is in a cast, as it has been for several weeks now, only it now itches so badly I can barely control the urge to scratch it. The doctor told me that itching is a sign the bone is almost done healing. A fact for which I'm grateful as the summer heat is already plaguing the Georgia coast.

I am so bored waiting in this office. The clock reads 2:31. I've been sitting in this uncomfortable chair since 1:56. School lets out at 2:45, so I can't imagine waiting for much longer.

The front office is as bland as can be expected. The walls have generic office art, the cabinets and the counters are steely grey, and the chairs are blue plastic and unyielding. The ticking of the wall clock is grinding on my nerves, a doleful sound loud in this quiet place.

"Penny? Mrs. Christopherson will see you now," Mrs. Smithson says.

I breathe in relief. Stiffly, I get up from the plastic chair and head for Mrs. Christopherson's office. She looks up at me from behind her enormous and cluttered desk. Mrs. Christopherson is in her late forties or so. Her hair is not greyed but there is age in her eyes. She is young enough however to have fairly progressive ideas about education. She is also new to the area, a fact which often works in her favor in my mind.

She sets aside her work when I come in, adding papers to an already precarious stack on one corner of her desk. She gestures to an old wooden chair, probably here since the founding of the school, and I sit again in an uncomfortable seat.

"Miss Williams," she begins, "it has been brought to my attention you may have been experiencing some difficulty in your home life."

My mind flickers through several possible people who could have spoken to her on my behalf, but I can't pin down who it would have been. Maybe she just noticed my change in demeanor.

"What do you mean?" I ask, trying to fish for more information.

Mrs. Christopherson leans back in her chair and studies me for a moment. "Well," she begins, "your grades have slipped, for a start. You started the year with nearly straight A's. You are barely pulling a C average. You have missed a lot of classes."

I grind my teeth. My grades have slipped because my parents have pulled me out of school on a regular basis to confine me at home or force me to meet with religious people from around the state. My grades are good—when I'm here to participate.

"Everyone's grades slip sometimes," I answer, barely hiding my annoyance.

"True," Mrs. Christopherson says. "But you have missed enough classes that you cannot miss anymore if you wish to complete seventh grade."

I swallow. I had no idea it had gotten that bad.

The impact must have shown on my face. She leans forward and adds, "And there is the matter of your injuries."

For some time I have been aware of rumors around the school that I am being abused at home or something. Mostly my injuries consist of bad bruises or a level of soreness that affects my ability to walk straight. The injury she is pointedly staring at is my broken arm.

For months I have been training my power under the tutelage of Altair and Ikthiel and Harilsen. Their lessons often leave me exhausted and beaten up to a degree. My parents are so against my craft that I started sneaking out in the dead of night to be trained. Recently, a poorly executed attempt at flying led to me falling forty feet and landing on my wrist. Altair caught me about three feet above the ground, but not soon enough to prevent a break. I had gone three days before the school nurse realized I was injured and sent me to the ER for X-rays. It was there that they found the hairline fracture in my left ulna. I couldn't find a reasonable answer to how I got the injury, so I simply said I fell. Mrs. Christopherson's questions made me wonder if it was drawn to her attention at that time.

"I fell," I say simply. "I was being stupid and I fell down the stairs." Even to my own ears it sounds like a lie.

Mrs. Christopherson's eyes narrow.

I let out a tight breath. I realize a little bit of the truth might benefit me here.

"I have a friend," I say. "His name is Altair. I sneak out at night to see him. My parents can't know." I look at her pointedly.

She nods, encouraging me to continue.

"We were out a few weeks ago," I say. "I took a bad step, Altair caught me, but my wrist hit the ground the wrong way. I thought I was fine, but it was fractured." I shrug. "It was just dumb luck."

Mrs. Christopherson doesn't relax at my self-effacing remark. Instead she seems more concerned. I think about my words and wonder if those are exactly the words abused people say to thwart any inquiries. I just can't abide the possibility of someone coming around my house and questioning my family. I probably would seem abused, but that isn't what worries me. I can't let anyone find out about my craft. I am under strict instructions to protect my Witch's secret as much as possible.

"Please," I say, "don't tell my parents. They think I just had a minor fall coming home from school. They would kill me if they think I was sneaking out to see a boy." I blush when I say it. The blush can only help my case.

Mrs. Christopherson's features soften slightly.

"Do you feel safe, Penelope?" she asks.

A knot forms in my stomach. "Yes," I lie. I have not felt safe in over two years.

She nods, studying me. "It seems to have been resolved," she says. "But I advise you tell them yourself about this boy. And I advise you to be more careful. Stop sneaking out at night. Your safety is important."

A lump fills my throat. So much of me wants to just confess everything I'm going through right then and there. But I know I can't. I know I don't have anyone to talk to and I can't really tell anyone.

"I'll be careful," I say. "Altair felt bad about my arm. I'm not sneaking out anymore."

*At least not that way*, I add grimly. My flying lessons would resume next week.

"How long are you in the cast for?" Mrs. Christopherson asks.

"About another month," I answer. "Maybe less. They said it's healing fast."

The steely woman nods and continues to study me. "Do you need any help in the meantime?"

I decline the extra assistance. I have learned in the past two years the value of being invisible. And extra help would only draw attention to my situation. I am already struggling to hide from Lucy as it is.

"If you need to talk, my door is always open," Mrs. Christopherson says pointedly.

And in that moment I know I haven't fooled her for one second.

My heart pounds as I get up to leave.

"Come in Bryce," she calls past me.

I brush past her son Bryce Christopherson on my way out the door. Not even a glance can I spare him as I think over the whole conversation again and again in my mind.

How could I be so stupid as to mention Altair by name?

And how was I supposed to keep this hidden for much longer when my magic constantly threatened to out me at every second?

I rush out of the office and into the busy corridor of the middle school. The bell rings overhead and I feel it like an arrow through my body. A mild panic sets in and I rush to leave.

I don't feel safe anywhere anymore.

# 15

*NOW*

"Penelope."

The soft voice is louder to me than the voices yelling my name from afar. I feel warmth at the base of my skull where the worst blow landed. The pain subsides and I blink several times in the dim jungle light.

"Ikthiel?"

"Yes," he whispers. He helps me up to a sitting position and examines my various other bruises.

I realize what he has just done and my mind churns over the times in the past few years when I had been badly injured and in need of medical attention. Most prominently the broken arm stands out. Annoyance floods my body as I watch him examining my other injuries.

"I didn't know you could heal," I blurt out.

His dark eyes meet mine and for a moment I catch a flicker of regret from him. "I'm sorry to have concealed that from you," he says. "I've hidden a lot from you, I'm afraid."

I don't know how to respond to his remark. But I realize I don't have to. We are completely isolated at this moment on a remote planet deep in the jungle with people who don't know where I am or that he is here. And he chooses this moment to completely drop his shields.

"I see."

Those are the only words I could muster at the influx of information. We have not often communicated telepathically, not for lack of compatibility, but more for preservation of privacy. He also thinks I am too young to know his mind. But I know darkness and I know evil even at my age. And I often question if Ikthiel cannot be saved.

This moment is not one of those moments.

"I'm sorry," he whispers. What's worse is he is sincere. A demon who feels the need to apologize has done something terrible indeed.

"They will kill you if you do not bring it back?" I ask.

He places a clawed hand in mine and I can see through his predictor demon's eyes that he is telling the truth. There are two fixed futures to this choice: if he brings what they want, he is safe; if he does not, he dies.

"Do you consider me a friend?"

Ikthiel is surprised I asked the question. I'm not sure why. Despite our years of knowing each other, I wasn't sure until this moment that demons could even have friends.

He answers my question, "Yes."

"For my power?"

The answer to this one is more difficult for him to find. I suspected for years it is my power that attracts him to me. Maybe I'm just pessimistic like that.

"Not exclusively," he says. Again this is probably the most honest I have heard him be.

I narrow my eyes at him and decide to challenge him on this. "Name one thing you like about me besides my ridiculous power." I shift on the dirt and wince at the pain in my ribs.

"You're insightful," he says. "For a human."

Never in a million years could I have guessed his answer.

I hear voices calling my name from above us. I look around myself now and realize I fell a good long way down the volcano. The trees around me are larger and must have stopped my fall.

"I can't heal you," he says regretfully. "They would know someone was here."

I touch the back of my head, feeling the tenderness despite the complete healing there.

His face shows no emotion as he says, "That injury would have killed you if they didn't get down here quickly enough. I couldn't let that happen."

Either for my power or for me, I'm not sure. But it is enough.

"I need my power right now, for this," I say. "And you will not deplete me if I do not want you to."

"I won't need to. Even a tenth of your power would be far more than we could ever use."

I pause.

"Can you assure me it will not be used to kill?"

"No."

I feel a queasiness come over my stomach. Demons are asking for my power to do something I only vaguely understand from Ikthiel's mind. I trust Ikthiel, but I do not know the other five. I could not possibly trust them enough for this.

But then my thoughts circle back in me and I hear again what I just thought.

I *trust* Ikthiel. By now I know Ikthiel could have taken my power, with or without my knowledge or consent. His life depends on this, but instead of taking it he is asking for it.

Could I just be justifying his actions to myself? Could I be justifying my own?

I choose not to overthink it.

I nod once.

"I swear I will help you in every way I can for this," he whispers.

A tiny smile, somewhat painful on my bruised cheek, crosses my face. "I can only imagine." I pause but then say, "You should go if you don't want them to know you were here."

His clawed hands squeeze my scraped fingers. Then my fingers are grasping at nothing but the humid air.

A few moments pass while I absorb what I just agreed to and everything Ikthiel said to me. Many times will I have to go over what I heard from his mind. The demon's predicament is harsh to say the least.

Finally I take a breath and call out to the voices aloft, "I'm here!"

No doubt they will think I was unconscious this whole time.

It is our ta-kef-ee guide who finds me first. I hear the strange metallic feathers rustling above me as he comes down through the foliage. He is taller than I am by a foot or so. He kneels beside me and checks me up and down, his delicate claws probing my bruises on my legs and arms. I am dressed in shorts and a tank top for this ridiculous jungle.

"Your injuries are bad," he says simply. I agree with him. I'm afraid my left ankle is sprained, maybe broken. "I will carry you into Berkaan. We have healers there."

The Takeef are not chatty.

"Thank you."

He picks me up like I weigh nothing to him and swings me onto his back. His long arms are really wings and his legs are a second set for gliding. His tail is broad and covered with more metallic feathers. I wrap my arms around his neck and I am very close to his scaled head. The position is painful. I grit my teeth.

The ta-kef-ee takes off and I get hit in the face a few times by leaves from the canopy. Then we clear the deep layer of leaves and he flies us over the forest toward the glow of Berkaan. The view is incredible but the flight is so bumpy that I can't really enjoy it.

"You do complain a lot," the guide says.

I feel a blush spreading across my cheeks. Today has tried my patience so much that my usual self-control with my thoughts has slipped.

"I apologize if I have offended you," I say robotically through a clenched jaw.

"Your reputation precedes you," he answers. "And my name is Fahum. I know you have forgotten."

Annoyance coils around my midsection. I do not remember any of their names, any of the group I am working with today. My commissions bring me into contact with too many people to remember all of their names. It is a poor excuse, but I can't find the energy to change that about myself. Since starting at the

Academy, I have met hundreds of people. I don't always remember all of their faces.

Fahum doesn't say anything else. I know the Takeef are telepathic, but I don't even bother trying to hide my thoughts. The pain spreading throughout my body is getting the better of my control. My ankle is throbbing, most likely swelling in my hiking boot.

"We will land in a moment," Fahum says.

He flies over several structures. I hesitate to call them buildings. They resemble glorified nests, tall structures that seem conducive to a flying species. A tall central "tree" structure becomes Fahum's main target. He circles once to slow down and then swoops up to a midlevel branch. Several ta-kaf-ee are waiting for us on the landing, no doubt because Fahum called ahead.

Several claws gently take my arms and carefully remove me from Fahum's back. He cordially holds very still for them. I am cradled by feathered arms and taken to an interior part of the nest.

They set me down on a cushion woven of fibers. One ta-kef-ee bends over me, another male I think, and he examines my injuries.

"Your ankle is broken," he remarks. "I need to remove your boot. It will hurt."

He is not kidding. He cuts through the laces sending a jolt through my ankle. I flinch and cry out as the boot slips over the swollen ankle. He waits a moment before going after my sock. I feel the blood drain from my face as the sock squeezed over the swollen mangled bone. The whole world swirls overhead and I am grateful I am lying down.

They examine my foot for a moment. I struggle to sit up on my elbows and I can see how bad it looks. The skin is a deep red, the ankle turned at an odd angle. I curse Ikthiel silently for leaving me with such a bad injury. Part of me wonders why he was unwilling to let anyone know he was here.

I look up and meet the healer's eyes. Belatedly I remember the Takeef are mind-readers. The horror of what I have just thought flashes through me and is reflected in the healer's eyes.

"I will keep your secret," the healer whispers. "My people are not so judgmental of demons as Witches are."

The other healer squeezes my shoulder and murmurs that he will do the same.

Relief floods my body.

"I will heal you now," the healer says. "This is going to hurt." After a pause he adds, "The demon is more skilled than I."

The ta-kef-ee behind me gently uses my shoulders to pull me back into a lying down position. I relax under his touch. Then I feel the bone move in my ankle. Reflexively I cry out in pain. I can feel the power of the healer's touch coursing through my body. Tears fall unbeckoned from the corners of my eyes. Anger fills me and I rush to push it down. The Takeef should not see that side of me.

Eventually, after an age of time it seems, the pressure on my ankle eases up. I can move my toes again without feeling the vice grip of pain that I felt before.

"Easy now," the healer says. The one holding my shoulders releases me, but continues to wait just in case.

It is at this moment that the Thell volcano chooses to make itself known.

The quake that sends a tremor through all of Berkaan threatens to topple the tower I am in.

"Hold tight!" the warning is called out from above.

All around the healing tower a flurry of wings shows the rapid departure of millions of Takeef. I do not even fathom how they can fly in such density and proximity to each other. My heart races as the nest tilts dangerously. I can't even stand much less *fly*.

One healer grabs me, slings me onto his back, and takes to the sky just as the tower begins to topple over.

We rise into the night sky. Dread fills me. Below us the destruction is apparent. No matter if we are able to halt the volcano now, the result of our delay is clear.

Around us the night air echoes with the voices of dying.

# 16

*NOW*

Several hours later I stand in the Witch's circle below the Thell volcano. Fahum is holding me up. He is not a Witch; he is only here to assist with anything we might need. My leg is not completely healed, but with Fahum's help I am able to stand on it well enough to get through this job. And we need to get this completed. The few hours that followed the last eruption scared me to the core and demonstrated why my power is so useful.

The diagram is simplistic as it lights up in front of me. A series of circles overlapping circles is all that is required to calm a volcanic interruption. Planets respond well to simplicity, things like gravity and pressure. No need to complicate this work.

I wait impatiently as Witch after Witch snakes an appendage into a circle in front of them. My circle blinks in front of me, the last one to be activated. Always the last one. Fahum's wing loops around me, stabilizing me while I try to reach my hand into the loop. I feel it clamp down on my wrist and I drop all my shields.

The flood of power I throw into the spell matrix blinds all the Witches tied into it. I feel it fly out of me as if I held back a dragon and for the first time it is stretching its wings. Fahum is struggling to hold onto me, to help me keep my footing. His wing shakes with the energy surrounding me now.

Where did all this power come from?

Amidst this power, focusing my mind is like trying to keep my footing on shifting sands. I realize the spell must be waiting for the execution word. Rather than wait for one of the other Witches to be composed enough to speak the word, I say it. The execution word burns in my throat. Power like dragon's fire exhales out of me as I let go of the spell matrix.

Nahnu-beit shudders.

For a moment I think the planet might be trying to reject the correction. A tug-of-war takes place between the spell matrix and this tiny, volatile planet. Every shove and kick from the rebelling planet results in a controlled shudder of the ground below us. But the matrix immediately corrects the activity and digs deeper into the matter of the planet. Though I can feel the shudders through my connection to the spell, I know the planet is stable, is still.

And then the Thell volcano exhales a puff of steam as the matrix reaches the planet core.

Like so many threads of a net, I feel it encircling the planet core as if it were my own heart at the center. Nahnu-beit stops struggling.

The matrix flames out and my power drops away.

My limbs go out from under me like a puppet with its strings cut. Fahum catches me. I struggle to keep from passing out.

The Witches around me blink in response to their sight returning. Every one of them glances at me in turn. Astonishment rolls off of them in waves and I know I have exceeded all expectations once again. I can even feel the tell-tale fear in reaction to my power.

I don't know how much time passes with the Witches watching me as I watch them. But I feel my mind beginning to fade as exhaustion begins to take over.

"I will fly Miss Williams back to the transport site," Fahum says. "You can all find your way back?"

The Witches ascent to the arrangement. Fahum swings me onto his back and a moment later we lift off. I see the faces of the Witches upturned as we fly overhead.

A moment passes before Fahum speaks. "I did not know you

have power like that."

"Oh," I say. "I was here to fuel the spell."

"Is that all you do?"

My mind races thinking of all the possible responses. But all I say is, "No."

I am often asked to do nothing but loan my power out. I certainly can do more than that. Altair's power I have used many times to jump back and forth. Ikthiel believes I can use the same techniques demons use to keep from needing an atmosphere as directly as I do now. What limitations could I really have if I have it in me to do those things?

Fahum says, "You should embrace your differences."

I hold tight to him as he veers around the far hills of Thell. The open plains on the southwest side of the island come into view.

"My people value differences," he continues as he swoops downward towards the trees. "The particularly different and the especially unique have saved our home many times."

In his native language, the words to which I am listening, I hear him say "nahnu-beit" though the translation matrix changes it to "our home." Unlike Earth which has a name rooted in mythology or religion or an old language, the Takeef always refer to their planet as Our Home. As if that is the name. I think then the kind of value they place on the people who have helped save them in the past. Their heroes are those who gave for the greater good, for the good of the people. The Takeef believe in the power of home.

"Yes, we do," he says, following my train of thought.

"But I am often met with fear or anger," I explain, thinking of the researchers on Widdershin or my own family back on Earth.

"Not everyone feels how we do," Fahum says. "We are not a warlike species, so we favor peaceful appreciation over aggressive hate."

Earth could learn a thing or two from the Takeef.

"Sometimes we feel we have a lot to teach other worlds," he answers my thought.

"They must be willing to learn," I answer.

Fahum gives a throaty squawk of agreement. "In the meantime, do not be afraid of what you are. There is always some need for a Guardian," he says.

A question crosses my mind and for the first time I think to ask it. "Why do some species call us Guardians?"

He turns his head a bit. I have been leaning over his shoulder so I could hear him and this move lets his eye look at me directly. The yellow color and deep pupil study me for a moment.

"I wonder why they have not taught you the history of your own people," he says. "All Guardians know the story. It is the mantle which you all live up to."

At this point he is setting us down on the transit area, an open place with a single huge rock face underfoot. The rock provides stability to the transit squares—actually hexagons here.

I am too exhausted to ask him to tell me the story. But it occurs to me again how little I know of my own heritage, of my ancestry and ancient past. Fahum sets me down on a soft patch of vegetation resembling moss. I blink uncontrollably, trying to keep from falling asleep. The stress and anxiety from the past several hours finally catches up to me. Fahum waits with me for the rest of the Witch's circle to arrive.

I sigh deeply looking at the world around me. The forbiddingly dark green of the jungle no longer seems so uninviting.

"You can come back," Fahum says.

"Why?" I ask.

He looks down at me with his yellow eyes. "I know you think we would not welcome you because you were too late." I blink up at him. It is exactly my fear. "You were not too late, Penelope. Disasters happen. Our people carry on."

"I'm an awful person, Fahum," I say. "Why are you being so nice to me?"

He rests his wing over my shoulders, holding me up. "It is the awful people that need the most kindness." He looks at me with what I assume is amusement in his eyes. "And you need the most kindness of anyone I have ever met."

I roll my eyes.

Together we watch the time tick by and wait for the others to arrive. Before long I drift off without recognizing the time that has passed.

17



*NOW*

In the last hour or so, my legs have turned to jelly from the power I am putting out. I step off the platform in Firrl's lab and one of the telekinetics scoots a stool in my direction. I take a seat gratefully. Sometimes when I am working with the researchers, the tasks they have me do are so menial, so small that the drain on my power surprises me. Sheer power is easy. Precision is the difficult part.

As I am mulling over the philosophy of power and staring into space, a glass of ice cold water appears in the air in front of me. I take it and look over at Zymyhpmi and raise the glass in their direction. They lifts a tentacle and turns their stalk eye back to the monitor. I drink the water greedily.

"*Penny?*" Namawh's half-telepathic, half-melodic voice calls. "*Would you come sit with me for a moment, please?*"

I cross the room to the ever-polite Aix, a species of almost-corporeals whose matter constantly shifts into a pleasantly purple energy. Unlike the Feirlu I had worked with on Nahnu-beit, Aix do not feel the forces of magnetic fields. I don't understand their energy at all, which, unlike Feirlu, is not a type of plasma. The couple times I brushed the purple energy on accident it felt like a warm summer breeze.

Namawh gestures obtusely to a seat next to their lab bench.

The Aix's vivid green cattish eyes study the computer in front of them, though I am unable to read it from this angle. I set down the empty glass and it folds out of existence.

*"Now, I am reviewing some answers to the initial interview questions from when we first started,"* they explains. *"I will just verify them and then have you look over our findings."*

I nod in understanding.

Namawh begins by asking, *"You stated your family history includes no Witches for several generations?"*

"Correct," I answer. "The last possible Witch was five generations ago. I doubt the accuracy of it given the events of the time."

*"The Burnings,"* Namawh remarks.

"Yes."

*"And before then?"* they asks.

"I don't know," I answer. "The few Witches on Earth consulted about our history had no records before then."

*"Not your father's side."*

I grimace reflexively. "No" is all I say.

Namawh moves on and continues with the question list, going over my responses to when I found my power and how. And delving into my affiliation with demons—something the researchers are never judgmental about. When Namawh falls silent, I know we are almost done. As I sit waiting, my wrist piece buzzes with the alert of a new message. I don't check it right then as Namawh's green eyes turn to me. They turns the screen to face me and the display comes up.

Two diagrams fill the display. One is a pie chart dominated primarily by one color. The other looks like a line chart with multiple series on it. I squint at the script in the legends and read the standard Witch script with practiced familiarity. The pie chart is labeled "Power Affiliations" and the dominant color corresponds unsurprisingly with sheer power. The line chart shows generational presence of power affiliations, with the color corresponding to the same items on the pie chart. I look closer at the lines and read that the power color is at zero for many generations, only spiking up with the current generation: me.

Contrastingly, the yellow color representing "concealment" is high during those generations and low for the current generation.

"No power for all these generations," I remark.

"*About 750 generations, as we can tell,*" Namawh says. "*It could be longer, but that is the start of your genetic tree as we can tell from our records.*"

Ignoring the fascination that they have genetic records of Earth back that far, I point to the other affiliations on the pie chart. "What do these mean?"

Namawh adjusts the display to zoom in on the four other wedges. One is simply labeled "Other" with a list of possible constituents. The other three are "Concealment," "Adaptation," and "Space-time."

"*Almost all Witches from worlds like yours have a good amount of Concealment,*" they explains. "*We believe it is an evolutionary development for survival.*"

"What about 'Space-time'?" I ask. My knowledge of relativity is cursory at best.

"*Well, we're not sure why yet. But to give you an example, Altair's power is dominated by space-time, almost as much your as yours is dominated by power,*" they says.

My eyebrows go up. "You mean I could use his power instead of just using the spell matrix?"

"*It's possible,*" they acknowledges. Namawh pulls up the list of other affiliations. "*The most intriguing I think is this tiny sliver right here,*" they says. The one they points to is under the "Other" wedge and reads "Universal – Unclassified." One tiny appendage goes corporeal long enough for them to tap the word "Universal." A long list of affiliations fills the screen.

Glancing through the list a few words pop out at me. Most I gloss over because I don't know what kind of power that is. However, words like "supernova" and "nebular collapse" and "gravitation" I understand. And the possibility of one Witch controlling that kind of power is jarring to my sense of reality.

Then far down in the list I see one word: "edge." A filament of cold touches my soul thinking of the Edge.

*"So you see the possibilities are diverse,"* Namawh says, jarring me out of my thoughts.

"Yes" is all I can say.

The display shifts again as Namawh changes the format. They zooms in this time on the lifetimes graph and takes it out as far as they can go. The reddish spike representing my current life's power is exponentially high compared to the previous lifetimes. The vertical axis has a scale break in it to accommodate the higher peak. They taps the display again and another line overlays the graph in a contrasting pale blue.

*"This line represents the overall average of Witch power in the past generations,"* they explains. *"We did some analysis on your power compared to generational averages. We summed the average power for all generations back to your last known Witch ancestor."* The graph changes again, this time all the blue is stacked vertically next to my reddish spike. The blue spike is still shorter, but the difference is not as significant.

"What does that mean?" I ask, though I can probably guess.

Namawh looks at me with kind eyes and says, *"It seems we have an explanation of where your power comes from. You have a concentration of power equivalent to the missing power from generations in your family as well as a significant portion of your own."*

For a moment I pause. I think about this. And I break down laughing so hard the rest of the lab goes silent at my response. I'm laughing so hard that tears start forming and I can't catch my breath. Zymyhpmi conjures a tissue and I take it gratefully unable to stop laughing while I wipe my eyes.

After a few minutes of this, Firrl finally asks, "Alright, what's so funny?"

I'm fanning myself trying to calm down enough to speak. "Well you saw it," I answer. "There's been no Witches in my family for generations, but you're telling me I have all of that power?"

*"Yes,"* Namawh answers, still confused.

"My family *hates* that I am a Witch," I continue. "You don't know the half of what they did to me when they found out." I crack up again, laughing but more controlled this time. "It's their own fault! I have all of their power too. My mother and probably my brother were Witches without knowing it."

"*Probably.*"

"Well it's what I've been saying for years." I wipe my eyes feeling vindicated at long last. "I was born with this power and I got it from them!" I shake my head. "If there's anyone who should be shunned, or sent to Christ camp, or *who should be beaten for being a Witch . . .*" the last one makes me shake my head and makes Namawh's eyes go wide as they look at Firrl for confirmation. "Well no one should have that. It's no one's fault. My family are Witches. They may never know that, but it feels good for me to know."

I'm on my third tissue by this time. While wiping my eyes, I can feel the research group exchanging glances. I realize two things. This is the first time any of them, perhaps anyone on Widdershin, has heard me laugh. I haven't had a good reason to laugh and it felt surprisingly good. The other thing I realize is regarding my history. No one has any real details about what I've gone through. They may have briefed Firrl before she took me on, but other than that I don't think any of them knew.

I open my hand filled with used tissues. Zymyhpmi makes them poof out of existence and conjures another glass of water.

Firrl walks over and hands me my wrist communicator. "It went off a few minutes ago."

"Thanks," I say. There's a message from Alicia Cole asking me to come to the administrative meeting. I put a finger to the message and think out my reply. It appears in text and I tap the send button. I let them know where I am and that it will be a little while before I get back up there.

"Let me walk you back up," Firrl says.

I shake my head. "No, I'll be fine," I say, setting down the empty glass. "Thank you for showing me that, Namawh."

The Aix's cat eyes almost smile. "*You're welcome, Penelope Williams.*"

Hearing my full name doesn't bother me for once.

I wave a cursory farewell to the rest of the research group and head for the surface. My mind keeps going over all the things I saw in the single chart. The biggest, most looming reality is the question of how my life would be if I had known from the start about my power. How would my life be if my family had known? How would it be if they had held the power themselves?

Watching Tethys go by the train windows, I wonder if I would even be here now. I don't know what day it is back on Earth. I doubt it's summer. Not enough time has passed.

Almost an hour after getting her message, I step through the doors of one of the small administrative buildings off the quad. The building houses most of the offices for envoys around the galaxy. Alicia Cole's Widdershin office is here. For a moment I wonder where her Earth one is, if she even has one.

I knock on the door to her office and poke my head in. She has no secretary. Her fourth floor windows look out over winter Widdershin and the cold weather out there. I open up my jacket in the warmth of the room. Alicia Cole's office resembles that of a professor. The clutter does not seem disorganized, just haphazard. Earth artifacts collect dust on every shelf and on her desk. A tiny globe of Earth spins idly next to her nameplate. Behind her a map of Earth has pins in it.

"Have a seat," Alicia says softly.

I take the only open seat, a rickety metal chair that reminds me of the old wooden one in Principal Christopherson's office. For a moment I feel like I am in trouble.

"I got a communique from the Deputy Head Witch of Earth," she begins. "There's some news you need to be privy to."

I wait without response. Suddenly the laughter of an hour ago feels millennia in the past.

Alicia studies me and then says, "I'm afraid Rebecca Whitney has passed away." She lets the words sink in for a moment. I'm not quite processing what she has said. "I know you two still kept in touch," she continues. "I thought you would want to read my deputy's letter and the obituary that will be posted tomorrow."

My voice seems to have left me. All I can do is nod.

She hands a tablet over with an image of a physical, typed

letter. I read it but the words, English words, feel jumbled. I swipe to the next image and the obituary is there. Both the Earth obituary and the Widdershin posting form paragraphs stacked one on top of the other. I can't seem to understand the words right now.

"Can I keep this?" I croak out.

Alicia nods sympathetically. "Penelope, I'm so sorry. I truly am." She pauses. "Can I get you anything? Anything at all?"

I shake my head. I am holding on by a thin tendril of myself.

"Can I go?" I ask.

Alicia nods. "Of course," she says. "But please don't hesitate to reach out if you need anything."

"I will," I say even though I feel it's a lie. There are few people I would reach out to at this point.

I leave her office without another word. I'm standing on a transit square, hugging the tablet to my torso, when I realize I haven't closed my coat. Then I am gone from Widdershin with hardly a thought and I find myself standing on Imfra-Rega's plateau on Kaldreesa.

For a few minutes I can't move. The house sits peacefully before me, empty at this hour of the day except for Imfra-Rega herself. She sees me and comes walking across the plateau, slowly closing the distance to me. I'm not sure why I came here. I'm not sure I feel safe enough to come here, but this is the last place I let myself grieve.

Imfra-Rega comes close to me and looks at my face. "Penny?" she asks, concern in her voice.

"Rebecca Whitney is dead." I hug the tablet closer to me as if it will give me some solace. The only human who gave me a safe home on Earth has died. I turned my back on my homeworld when I left it months ago. But here, now, with my last safe guardian dead back on Earth. Now I feel the sense of loss I should have last year. I feel the disconnect from Earth. I feel Rebecca Whitney's wisdom, her quiet caring, her respect all slipping away.

Imfra-Rega places a foreclaw on my shoulders and guides me back to the house. We are not far and she turns me around to set on the bottom step. I sink into it, feeling the weight of my winter jacket around me in this warm desert world.

I look again at the tablet, this time reading the worlds for real. She died today. I look at the date at the top of the letter. January 25th. Today is January 25th back on Earth. Today is my birthday. Today I turn fourteen.

How fitting that today I would experience both laughter and tears.

And I am crying now. Crying for the old Witch who took me in. The Witch who gave me space to live and freedom to roam. Lucy often referred to her as my great-aunt and I never corrected her. If anything, she was my only family. The only family who trusted me.

Imfra-Rega wraps a forearm around me, gently holding me. The tears are silent but they blur my vision completely. I hug the tablet close as Imfra-Rega holds me. I'm not sure who I'm crying for more: Rebecca Whitney or myself. I'm not sure it matters.

"We hold you safely," I hear Imfra-Rega whisper. I believe her.

## 18

*BEFORE*

"I didn't forget it was your birthday," my brother's voice says from the doorway of my bedroom. "Neither did they."

I stare at him from my desk chair. I try to remember the last time we have spoken at all, much less without our parents present. For one strange moment I realize I am struggling to remember his name.

The coldness in my ten-year-old brother's eyes was not there the last time we spoke. It was not there the last time my parents yelled at me. It was not there when we were children laughing and playing together before the power came, before the Witches knew me. Before. He stands fifteen feet from me, but he might as well be in Scotland.

"I heard them talking," he says. "They said you didn't deserve to be celebrated. Mom said she wish you'd never been born."

The words should hit me like a blow. But they fall flat. In the past two years, I have learned just how unfeeling my family can be. Just how intolerant they can be with something they don't agree with.

"Why are you still here? Why don't you just go away?"

I just stare at the person who used to be my brother. I stare at the person who used to think I was special and looked up to

116

me. I don't know him anymore. Silence is my only response to him.

"I wish you would just die," he says with venom in his words. "No one wants you here."

No one. Not even me. I don't want to be here anymore. The silent admission stings.

Anger flares in me for a moment. Without thinking I glance at my bedroom door and it flings shut in my brother's face.

"*I'm telling Dad!*" he shrieks from the other side of the door.

I'll probably regret doing that. But not right this second. Flexing my power even minimally feels good.

Ikthiel appears in the corner of my room, behind the door jam. A scolding look fills his face. I roll my eyes as far as I can.

"Be careful, Penelope," is all Ikthiel says before he disappears again.

I stand up and look out the window. Thinking about the door shutting in my brother's face, a smile curls my mouth.

Happy birthday to me.

19

*NOW*

"We have lost contact with the Marquis Delta Belt regional group," the latest Head Witch in a long line of Head Witches says to the room. However, this time, different from other times, my focus is unwavering.

Ikthiel stands to my right and Altair stands to my left. I am wearing Witch's armor similar to what I had seen Ikthiel wear many times before. Today is not the usual commission.

We are across a large circular table from the Head Witch who in this case (atypically) is a version of human. I know there are several cousin species to human out there in the galaxy, but I had not met one until today.

Qidan Durmark surveys the two dozen Witches in the room as if he were a teacher making sure his students are paying attention. He is human enough, but his eyes are nearly completely pitch black, his skin an ashy grey, and his hair very short to almost baldness. Then there is the matter of his height. He is nearly as tall as Harilsen, towering above me at almost seven feet. I barely come up to his elbow when I stand next to him.

"We suspect the Reeturs have cut off all communication," he continues looking over the starmap projected above the table in the middle of us. I am positioned right at the table across from

118

him, probably because I am shorter than everyone else here.

The past few months have been hectic. I barely had time to breathe after Rebecca Whitney's death almost three months ago. Though I stayed on Kaldreesa for a few days, I did not take time to grieve. The Academy would have given me more space, but I decided staying busy was better. As usual, I threw myself into my work.

A month ago, I went through my first comprehensive exams. When I passed, I moved into the second level of training at the Academy, what would have started during my sophomore year of college. My work became intensive and hands on.

The main administration at the Academy took my advancement as an opportunity to put me in the field in more delicate situations. No more star fixing for the time being. In the past month I have seen more of the local galactic cluster than I thought possible. It feels like every other day I am sent to another corner of the universe to interact with new people whose names I never remember. It was all slowly becoming a blur.

Ikthiel shifts next to me. I glance at him out of the corner of my eye. He is tense. We are dealing with demon-converts. The Delta Belt is a significant star-forming region in the Marquis Galaxy, known on Earth as the Pinwheel Galaxy. This spiral arm we are in has been in turmoil since a supernova a few years ago. It was not so close to cause real harm to the Delta Belt, but the affected region in the Gamma Belt housed several trillion people, all of which were either killed or displaced due to the event. The influx of refugees caused chaos in the Delta Belt and lead to the uprising we were sent here to deal with. Xenophobia infected the region and fighting broke out between the refugees and the native species.

The trouble with the Marquis Delta Belt increased to the point the heads at the Academy lifted the ban on the information. They briefed me a week ago about what Altair told me months ago on Kaldreesa. The past few months the Reeturs gained significant ground, their forces in the area increasing. Witches refusing to renounce their sparkpoints have been executed with prejudice. Every person in their path either bows to their power or is killed for resisting.

My attention remains focused on Head Witch Qidan. I wonder inwardly if he dislikes having to consult with amateurs like me. More than half of the squad of us have been in combat before. Witches have turned to war when necessary. The history I studied as part of my Witch's exams last month told me about the last one, almost two centuries ago. Hopefully, this will not be like that.

"Miss Williams," Head Witch Qidan says, "we need you to provide power, but I also understand you are developing a shield."

"Yes, I am," I say, the surprise registering in my voice. This is probably the first time a Head Witch has asked me about something other than power.

"I suggest you use it as much and as widely as you can," he says. His gaze casts around the room to the others and he adds, "Do not rely on Miss Williams to protect you. That is too great a burden even for the Powerhouse. Protect and defend yourself. The Reeturs and their allies will not spare us because we are Witches."

A murmur runs around the room at his warning. Head Witch Qidan does not pull punches. And he is correct. While I am working on a shield, I would not likely be able to protect more than a few people at a time. I roll my shoulders to release the tension building up there. Out of the corner of my eye, I see Ikthiel glance at me. I clench and unclench my jaw. The nerves are getting to me. There is an abundance of tension in this room.

"Our main mission," Head Witch Qidan continues, "is to locate our fellow Witches and provide rescue. We are not to engage the Reeturs except in defense."

A murmur runs through the room at his words.

Head Witch Qidan raises his hand for quiet. "I know, I don't like it any more than you do," he says. "But the Reeturs will do anything to trigger a sparkpoint—*especially if it means the Witch's death*. Their mission is to eliminate pre-spark Witches. Do not give them the chance to do that."

My throat goes dry at his words. The background information on the Reeturs turned my stomach and to hear it confirmed only unsettled me more. Sparkpoints can and often do require the death of the Witch to enact their full power at the moment of need. Rebecca Whitney living through her sparkpoint is not exactly a novelty. Many Witches do survive their sparkpoint, but the psychological toll is marked.

Mrs. Whitney told me over a year ago when explaining it, "Finding your way again after you have spent your power feels like coming back from the dead. The universe feels like a disconnected place and your power is a shadow of what it once was."

I feel a pang thinking of the wisdom she bestowed upon me. I didn't understand it at the time and maybe I still don't. But the warning not to allow a sparkpoint reinforced both what Mrs. Whitney said and what I read in the Reetur's background. In denying their own sparkpoints, the Reeturs retain much of their power though they lose something of themselves. This twisting of the soul makes them formidable and dangerous. Eventually it can twist the Witch into a demon.

I feel Ikthiel's gaze on me again. One look at him and I know from his expression he has been following my thoughts. And then the question comes to mind that I had not asked myself completely. Was Ikthiel a Witch a long time ago?

Ikthiel shows no reaction, reveals no answer.

My gaze goes back to Head Witch Qidan. I set aside the questions I have for another time and place.

The star map changes in front of me. The view zooms in to the region we are hiding in and then shows a relative distance to our target system. Each location is labeled in the scratchy universal Witch script. We are hidden on a sizeable asteroid called Unosa. Our destination is two systems over, a planet called J'Phonk. Like Widdershin J'Phonk houses a research center, but it does not have the training facilities Widdershin does. The planet is mostly non-Witches. In terms of Witch strongholds, this is a small outpost and not a major hub.

Head Witch Qidan details a mission plan that largely goes

over my head. I have only minimal tactical training and no experience. My position will be central to the group, protected on either side by Altair and Ikthiel, further circles of Witches around me past them. Altair will jump the entire group to a remote location on J'Phonk while I power his jump.

Ikthiel is here to provide demon senses, the kind of sense that can pick out a turned Witch from a great distance. In the same way a Witch can always recognize another Witch, demons know each other immediately. This is perhaps why Ikthiel is nervous. I know from his roundabout discussions of them that demons are rarely if ever friendly—even to each other. And Ikthiel is probably a traitor.

"I am a traitor," I hear his thought-voice say in the back of my mind. I glance at him and he nods at me once. "At least most demons see me that way."

"Why keep working with Witches?" I think back at him.

There is a pause. Then I get an image I have seen in his mind before: me as a ten year old child lifting every boulder in a field, more than a construction crew could move in a week. And another image I know: Altair appearing for the first time in our universe, a manifestation that looks nothing like his unusual teleportation. And the third image he shows me is unfamiliar but I can guess: a female demon glaring at him, threatening him with her posture and stance. The image alone sends a shiver down my spine.

So it's simple. Demons are simple. Power. Unique capabilities. And danger. The three things that keep Ikthiel on the Witches' side.

"It seems simple," his thoughts say. "But of course it's more complex than that."

But I know that already. Ikthiel is my friend. Friendship complicates everything.

Head Witch Qidan's voice snaps me back to the moment. "Any last minute preparations you need to make, make them now," he says. "It could be hours before we return. Plan accordingly. We leave in ten minutes."

With that the meeting is over. Murmured conversation

circulates the room. In the back of my mind, a burble of not-quite-heard thought circulates as well. I turn to Altair and Ikthiel and they nod.

"Is your atmosphere set?" Altair asks. He is wearing a portable atmosphere similar to mine, not surprising since we have the same breathing requirements. J'Phonk's atmosphere contains little to no oxygen and barely any pressure. It barely qualifies as an atmosphere.

"Yes," I answer with a glance at Ikthiel. He has been teaching me off and on to breathe without the apparatus. It is just a backup for now though.

Ten minutes seems like an eternity. I go over the specs for my shield again and again in my mind. The complexity of the matrix overwhelmed me the first time I used it. The base shape forms a geodesic dome and each section, each panel, fractals into intricate patterns. Each panel describes a different subset of powers or objects, the things that could present danger out there.

"Time to go," Head Witch Qidan calls out. I had gotten through about half of my shield.

As one the mass of Witches moves toward the large transit circle at the back of the room. The ring blinks in a holding pattern, waiting for activation till the signal is given. As planned I am stationed in the center with Altair and Ikthiel on either side. Head Witch Qidan is on the outer ring as most Head Witches would be. They take their responsibility seriously.

Head Witch Qidan nods once at Altair and then turns to face outward from the group. I feel a tug on my power. Briefly my vision goes dark. When it clears, the landscape of J'Phonk fills my view from horizon to horizon. The sight of it makes my stomach drop.

As expected my portable atmosphere kicks in to give me some extra oxygen. It doesn't help. I still feel that something is off.

All around us the ground is a bleak grey-brown color filled with dust and stone and absolute desolation. Nothing grows here. I don't know why I expected it to. But here, where people live, I did expect *something*. The vast emptiness reaches for each horizon. We are standing on a short plateau and the cliff drop off obscures our sight of the near ground below. In the distance ragged cliffs and razor-sharp mountains reach for the sky at the too-close horizon.

Even with the extra air helping me I can still feel the void around me, the slight tug hinting at the near vacuum. Cold bleeds through even with the extra layer protecting me. I am grateful the Witch's uniform is designed to protect against the cold. The Witch's armor over it certainly does little to protect against the cold.

"Are we in the right place?" a Witch next to Head Witch Qidan whispers.

Head Witch Qidan checks the coordinates on his wrist monitor and nods.

The pit in my stomach continues to sink further down. I don't know what it is, but something here feels off.

Ikthiel's focus remains on the horizon. His head swivels around, his posture becoming more tense. I follow his gaze to our right. As I see it, so do the rest of the Witches around me. Just past the outcrop below us, in the valley, a horde of people or Witches or demon-converts marches toward us.

A chill runs up my spine.

A high-pitched scream pierces the silence. To my left at the outer circle, a Witch is dead. Another flaming ball of energy flies up over the edge of the cliff. I watch it, entranced for a moment, and then I remember my shield. Can I guard against something so intangible? In my hand the spell matrix manifests itself, the complexities small at this size. That flare of power I felt on Nahnu-beit came again. The shield increases in size and range pushing out and out from me.

Not far enough.

This time we see the energy sphere fly up over the edge of the cliff. It almost seems to hang for a moment before arcing downward. The impact on the shield is immediate. I cannot control the cry that comes from me.

"What is it?" Altair asks in concern.

"I can feel it," I squeak out, panting to control my reaction to the pain.

I look and see the line of Witches outside the shield, vulnerable to the attack. One Witch whose name I didn't even bother to get, a tall alien of the same species as Harilsen, his power flares up, obvious in the blue fire suddenly pouring from his body. The glow around him a manifestation of his power expanding outward.

Then I realize what the horde below is: a decoy.

This is an ambush.

The thought must occur to everyone around me as well.

"Abort!"

Head Witch Qidan's voice is drowned out by the explosion.

I don't see the explosion.

Before I can react, I feel my shield collapse. Everything goes dark.

20



*NOW*

*"Penny."*

A whisper cuts through the dark and the murk in my head.

"Penny," the voice says again. I recognize Altair's voice.

I blink a few times and his face comes into view. I try to get up but he gently pushes me back down.

"Don't move," he whispers. "Ikthiel healed you but he says you had a concussion. The blast caught you from behind."

I wince at the reminder. Every joint aches. My skull feels like it's made of lead.

Around me is nothing but stone and dirt. We're in what looks like a shallow cave. I can't see much beyond Altair but the opening looks out on the open plain. The plateau in the distance glows with the persisting flame and heat of the explosion. It is obvious from this distance the battle is ongoing.

"Why are we here?" is the first question that comes to me.

"*Shh,*" Altair whispers frantically. "We're not well hidden. We were told to protect you. When the blast hit and you were knocked out, the shield went down." That much I figured. "Qidan told us to get you out of there. We've been watching them trying to evacuate, but they are still fighting."

"We should be helping them," I say, too loudly again, and I try to get up.

Altair again gently pushes me back down. "We're trapped," he whispers. "The Reetur's forces are all around us. I teleported as far as I could and it got us off the plateau."

"*What?*" is all I can say. "That's not possible." It shouldn't be. The pain in my head still a dull roar, I can feel a licking flame of anger in my core.

"Ikthiel thinks they are using a power dampener. It's an old demon's trap," Altair whispers.

"To prevent teleporting."

"Yes," Altair says. "The range can't be very big, but the moment we landed we were in it. He's looking for the source and testing the boundary."

"We should be helping," I repeat, this time quietly.

Altair nods but says, "Give yourself a chance to breathe. Ikthiel will be back in a moment."

As if on cue, the demon darts into the entrance of the cave. Ikthiel's eyes go from Altair to me. He immediately knees down beside me and places his hand behind my head. I feel his healing warmth there again. This is the second time he has prevented my skull from splitting open.

"How do you feel?" he whispers.

I almost say "fine" as a reflex but I consider for a moment. "Weak," I say, "but alert."

"I've done what I can," Ikthiel whispers, looking up at Altair who is watching the distance. "We have to get past the far ridge before you can get us off the planet." He points in the distance and my stomach drops. The distance is over a mile.

Hesitating, I ask, "What about the rest of them?"

"One thing at a time," Ikthiel says.

Altair looks back at me. "We need to go," he whispers. "They're getting closer."

"Can you stand?"

I nod gingerly. Altair and Ikthiel both pull me to my feet. Only now that I am standing can I see why they keep whispering. Boulders litter the field around us, most the size of small cars, marred with scorch marks and broken in ways nature does not break. The alcove Altair hid us in is just another scorched cut-out from an even larger boulder. Less than a quarter of a mile away, I catch glimpses of a knot of what I assume are Reeturs or their allies between the boulder flanking us.

"This way," Ikthiel whispers, leading us to our right.

The hairs on the back of my neck stand up as we creep through the boulders and the remnants of what was probably a battlefield. Ikthiel leads us between boulders, ducking down or crawling to the ground to stay out of sight. If I wasn't already filthy, I definitely was in the space of a few minutes. We manage for probably fifteen minutes, knees scraping on the ground or crouching to run between boulders. Then they see us.

A shout goes up from beyond the boulders to our left.

I don't see the fireball thrown at us, but I feel the heat of it as it narrowly passes over my head.

Ikthiel and Altair dive on me and crush me under their weight.

Everyone is talking and the Reetur's Witches are shouting but I can't understand a single word. The boulders to our right keep exploding. Panicking, I realize it is only a matter of moments before they decide to blow up the boulder concealing us.

One look at Altair and Ikthiel's faces and I see they have had the same thought.

Ikthiel says something to Altair and I don't understand him. For a moment I think it is the blasting sounds around us cutting out his voice. Then I see the look of confusion and alarm on Altair's face.

He turns to me and says, "*Penny—*," and the rest is nonsensical words, or maybe just words in his own language.

"*Can you understand me?*" I ask. Confusion on both their faces is enough answer.

With horror I realize what must have happened: *no Witch powers are working.* Not even the basic ones. Even the simplest spell matrix to allow us to communicate with each other.

Altair points to Ikthiel who nods. With a gesture like a cannonball launching and a point at Ikthiel's claws, Altair seems to get the point across. Carefully, Ikthiel peers around the side of the boulder. He stands up using the boulder as a shield.

Then I see demon's fire for the first time.

An arching line of blue and green and pink cuts through the sky from Ikthiel's claws in a mixture of violence and beauty. The fire's colors remind me of the aurora for just a moment. Screams coming from beyond the boulders squash any feelings of familiarity or nostalgia.

Again Ikthiel fires, the power releasing some demonic thing within him. His eyes burn a darker and more forbidding red than I have ever seen. I don't have time to think on it.

Altair pulls on my hand and drags me away though I have no idea where we can possibly hide in this mess. It is so dark now. Only Ikthiel's fire behind us casts an unreliable, flickering light. We run onward. Only once do I glance over my shoulder as Ikthiel stops firing. He is outlined in the darkness, running toward us now. His red eyes give him away.

I turn forward just in time to see the ledge. Not in time to stop.

A sudden steep slope falls away from us like the ground just chose to eat us. Altair's grip on my hand rips away from me painfully as we fall separately, tumbling through gravel and shards of rock on what feels like an endless slope. I hear a string of words I imagine to be swear words in Altair's native language, his voice getting distant and overpowered by the sound of rocks in my ears.

My left foot collides with an unseen boulder and I tumble to my right falling away from Altair's trajectory. I can't hear him shouting anymore. And I keep tumbling, feeling the bruises and the possible breaks cropping up.

Then just as suddenly I hit level ground.

My face pressed into the gravel underneath me, I struggle to put myself upright. A firm hand grabs my arm and drags me to my feet and pulls me away from the rockslide. The shock in my left ankle tells me it's at least sprained. I have no choice but to bear up under the pain of it as I put weight on it walk.

The person—it is definitely a person—who pulled me from the debris pushes me up against a sheer rock face and lets me slide to the ground.

"Stay here," a voice whispers and the figure disappears into the black darkness around me.

I don't question it. I gingerly feel my ankle and curse my lack of healing knowledge not for the first time, indeed not for the sixth by this point. It's tempting to take the boot off, but I know better by now. I feel pockets and the edges of my Witch's armor, not that it's any good anymore. Nothing is working, but nothing is missing either. The tiny knife along my belt at my back remains in place. I realize it's my only protection now.

A shadow reappears in front of me. The person crouches down and gingerly touches my ankle, much as I did.

"I think it's sprained," I whisper.

"Definitely sprained," the voice whispers back as she, for it's definitely a she, rolls the ankle gently. "Don't take your boot off."

"I won't," I answer.

Then it clicks.

"How can I understand you?" I whisper.

There is a pause. I feel the person shifting their weight as if fishing something from a pocket. The sound of a click and a sudden, dull green glow like that of a firefly or a dying glow-stick softly illuminates the face in front of me. The source of the light is smaller than a dime, and it's technology, not power. But it's enough to show me one thing: she is human.

"Are you from Earth?" she asks.

"Yes," I answer.

"America?"

"Yes. From Georgia." The words sound more foreign than any alien language.

I study the features of this woman as she studies me back. Middle age has hit her and the long, dark hair loosely tied back is streaked with gray. A feeling of recognition washes over me for a moment, but I feel it is her humanity that makes her seem familiar.

"Are you Madge?" I whisper. This is the only person this could be.

"Madge Matxino," she says, "Yes. And you are Penelope Williams."

"Yes," I whisper.

"Where is Altair?"

"He fell when I did but in the opposite direction."

There is concern in her eyes. "We'll have to find him and the demon," she whispers. "You and your lot can't stay here. You need to leave."

"I know," I whisper back. "It was an ambush."

She looks pained. "I tried to get word to Altair when I realized, but it was too late. The dampener was already in place." Madge hands me the light. "Is it just your ankle?"

"That's the worst," I say. The rest are just bruises and cuts I can deal with later.

"I'm gonna do my best to heal it a bit," she says. "It's not my power, you understand."

"Can you do that with the dampener?" I ask.

"Something like healing they usually forgot about," she says, before adding, "I hope."

She wraps her hands around my ankle, forming a kind of human shackle. Warmth flows from her palms and through the boot to the ankle. I can feel it in my bones. A few minutes pass and she lets got, panting with the effort. A line of sweat coats her brow even in this freezing landscape. She takes the light from me and stands.

"Put your weight on it."

With her help and the rock face behind me I get to my feet. The ankle is not completely healed, maybe just a few days older than it was. I can stand and probably walk on it, but not fast.

A wrinkle of concern folds Madge's brow. I can see her doing the math if we were discovered. "Stay close to me," she says. "I can't use the light away from here."

And with that we are plunged in pitch-black darkness again. Gingerly, I follow in her wake, trying not to further injure my ankle.

21



With the dampener in place, all my senses feel dulled. I can barely make out Madge's moving shape ahead of me. Somehow we make our way to the base of the slope where I fell. I follow Madge as she circles the rubble pile. There ahead of us I see a dark shape moving, silhouetted against the slightly less dark background. Madge freezes in front of me.

A single flame of demon fire illuminates from Ikthiel's claw.

Madge recognizes them at the same moment I do. She puts an arm around my back and helps me stumble forward. Even that little bit of walking and navigating the gravel sent dull pain up my leg.

"Her ankle is injured," Madge explains, passing me to Ikthiel. "See if you can help." She turns to speak to Altair, switching into a language other than English.

Ikthiel takes my arm over his shoulder and helps me sink to the ground. His demon claws wrap around my boot and again I feel healing energy flowing in. His is markedly stronger than Madge's, clearly not encumbered by the dampener in place. A moment later and I can move it without pain. Silently, I squeeze his shoulder to thank him. His eyes meet mine and I hear his thoughts in the back of my mind, "Please don't scare me again."

With Ikthiel's help, I get up. My leg feels as if it was never injured.

Standing again I tune in to what Altair and Madge are saying. A cold chill runs down my spine at the grave tone in their voices. The words make no sense, but the seriousness is unmistakable.

Madge catches my eye and explains, "At least two dozen dead so far. There will be more."

"Witches?" I ask, the strain evident in my voice.

She nods in response.

I realize Ikthiel's hand is still on my shoulder when he reaches his free hand out to Altair and Madge. They take it without hesitation. Through the contact he passes his thoughts.

In my mind I see the dampener, a dome arching over the whole area. He took the time to find the edge of it so we could get out, but he didn't stop there. He used the energy of the spell matrix to find the center, the control of it. With the dampener removed, Altair and I could evacuate all the Witches, dead or alive.

The spell matrix is so massive it is beyond my power to fuel alone. Five Reetur Witches—who else could they be—have their attention completely focused on keeping the matrix going. Even one losing focus would be enough to collapse the matrix. The only catch is that the Witches are over a mile from where we are now and there are guards around them.

Madge takes a long knife from her belt and nods at Ikthiel. Silently, Ikthiel tells me to stay with Altair when they get there so I could be ready to help him evacuate the Witches. For a moment, Madge sizes me up and then pulls a tiny knife from another spot in her person and hands it to me handle first.

"Don't cut yourself," she whispers.

"I'll try," I respond with as much sarcasm as I can muster in this dismal place.

Her mouth twitches in amusement.

With that we start to make our way up the gravel slope. A grueling fifteen minutes later and I fall into step beside Madge as we make our way across the surface. To our left and quite a distance away, I can make out the smoldering fires Ikthiel left burning. More disturbing is the plateau in the distance where I can still see the battle going on.

"When did you leave Earth?" Madge asks me.

I have to think for a moment to remember. "Almost a year ago." I look at her sideways and ask, "You?"

"About six years ago," she says. "I left everything behind."

"Why?"

She smirks at me sideways and says, "My family. They were into bad things."

I look at her for a moment and make a connection I suddenly think is obvious. "Do they know who you are?"

Her eyes glint in the odd lighting. "Only Altair and Ikthiel."

I glance at their backs, far enough ahead of me to be out of earshot. "That's why you hate the Reeturs."

Madge nods. "I don't regret leaving," she says. "Except for leaving my nephew. He was a good kid. I don't know how he is now."

"Who is your nephew?"

But Madge can't answer because at that moment we catch up to Altair and Ikthiel, hidden behind a boulder. We wait in silence, hidden from the passing contingent of Reetur hostiles. Once they are a safe distance from us, we move forward again. We don't talk anymore, just keep moving, hopping from spot to spot and hiding as we get closer to the spell matrix.

Finally, rounding a series of boulders, I can catch a glimpse of it. The complexity of the matrix is incredible if not entirely unexpected. The Witches running the matrix, I can just make out their faces in the energy coming off the matrix, but I can see they are totally focused. An ounce of lost concentration would collapse it.

Ikthiel's hand comes down on my shoulder. "Do you see the one to the right?" he asks.

I sight the one I think he means. He is human, tall and wiry. Longish dark hair is pulled back in a ponytail. His dark eyes, focused at this moment, swallowed by sunken sockets. The tips of his fingers show the curve of a pre-claw similar to Ikthiel's resting on my shoulder.

"He passed his sparkpoint. His nature fights him now,"

Ikthiel observed.

A shiver runs up my spine as I watch the Witch—former Witch really—pour their power in the matrix, the power itself wild and uncontrolled and vaguely demonic in nature.

"Be careful," Ikthiel says in the back of my mind. Then he moves forward to take point.

I go to hand Madge back her knife. She shakes her head and whispers, in English, "Keep it. You might need it."

"How can I find you again?" I ask.

For a fraction of a second she studies me, then she says, "You have enormous power. Use my name and you can get my attention." Then she leans forward and whispers in my ear, "My name is Mag-iwan Reetur."

I look at her for a moment then nod, slipping the blade back in my belt.

"Never trust a Reetur," she whispers. "Not even me."

With those parting words, she and Ikthiel move forward. I watch them go for a moment before they melt into the darkness.

Altair puts a hand on my shoulder, mimicking Ikthiel's typical pose. In the back of my mind I can sense Altair's thoughts but can't quite make them out. All I can sense is Altair's tension and his determination to be calm. I keep my gaze on the demonic Witch and the matrix. Beside him, a shadowy shape hovers, and I wonder for a moment if I am seeing a ghost.

My eyes are on the demonic Witch when it happens. I don't see Madge until the last second. The shadowy figure solidifies for a fraction of a second. The Witch's life goes out. Even from here the blade coming through his chest is unmistakable. Even from here I can see his death.

The reaction is immediate.

"Let's go," Altair says as the dampener goes down.

I lose sight of Madge in the influx of Witches who come on her. We have no time to deal with that. I just have to trust that she will take care of herself and Ikthiel will do what needs to be done.

Altair takes my hand and leads me at a run away from the area and toward the plateau. Do we need to go this far? He looks over his shoulder at me, a question in his eyes.

For just an instant I can see his doubts about my power, about my ability, about my willingness to give him what he needs.

My jaw sticks out with stubbornness. Even my friends doubt.

All my shields come down. It is like I am standing on Nahnubeit with Fahum holding me up. Only this time I am aware of my faculties and I am braced for the power as it flares up. More than before, more than ever, more than I could ever use in my whole lifetime. Still the Spark remains quiet.

As we run, as I concentrate on keeping my footing on the treacherous terrain and Altair raises a hand occasionally to deflect a plasma bomb or some other projectile, as we run closer to the Witches, I pour my power into him and give him everything he needs and more. He raises a hand to deflect another plasma bomb and it simply vanishes. The way he looks at me now, the surprise and the recognition, it is as if he is looking at a ghost.

Altair's grip on my hand tightens and I barely feel it as our realities shift. Suddenly we are on the plateau as if we took one step and the next was there. I catch myself and stop running. I don't let go of Altair's hand. Finally, I look at the ground. Something, emotion I thought long dead, catches in my chest and my throat.

All around us on the ground are bodies. Alien, human, some barely still here as their energy forms dissipate. So many. And those are the ones who weren't hit by an energy blast of some kind that vaporized them.

A sound comes out of me, I don't know what. I feel the pain surfacing now and the tears leak out for a moment. Horrifying to see the dead like this.

"Where's Qidan?" Altair says.

Frantically I search around us. So many bodies, so many faces whose names I don't know. So many people dead. Not just Witches. *People.* These are people dead all around me.

*There!* I hear Altair think clear as if he said it in English. He pulls me forward, stepping around and over bodies, halfway across the plateau where half a dozen Witches crouch behind a low outcropping. They see us coming. Fear mixed with hope fills their features. The emotion is unmistakable, though only one has a human face.

A swathe of blue fire arches up over the plateau and makes to rain down on us. Altair and I present an obvious target. Anger flares in me. How *dare* those traitorous bastards of Witches kill all these people and dare to try to kill us too?!

I barely glance up and the fire simple ceases to exist. Altair stares at me, feeling the anger and determination in me.

"We're getting everyone out of here," I say through clenched teeth. "Even the dead." I add, "And don't forget Ikthiel and Madge."

As if I summoned the demon with his name, Ikthiel appears to my left. He stares at me like I am a specter. "Madge left. She did what she needed to do."

Her words echo through me. *Never trust a Reetur. Not even me.*

Fine. Then I wouldn't trust her. Or anyone.

Qidan lays at my feet, held by a Witch who frantically tries to keep his injuries from killing him. That same shadowy figure I saw by the Reetur Witch hovers right next to his shoulder. I finally recognize the man is probably dying. He is probably going to die before we get off this rock.

I know it is a secret. Ikthiel meets my gaze. For a moment that feels like an eternity, he stares back at me in stubbornness and reluctance at using his healing abilities before strangers. Then he kneels down, pushes the Witch's hand aside, and pours power into Qidan. The moment Ikthiel makes the choice, the shadow flits away down to the valley below us.

The Head Witch looks up at me in astonishment. "You're glowing" is all he says.

Glancing down at my free hand I see he is right. Maybe the body can't contain the power past a certain point. I set the thought aside. I don't care.

"They stopped firing," one of the Witches observes. An eerie silence hangs over the plain now. The Reetur's forces below us, the Witches around us, Altair next to me: all seem frozen, immoving as if time itself holds its breath.

"What the—?" someone says.

Ikthiel shoots to his feet and looks up. I follow everyone's gazes, the Reetur's forces and the Witches. I look up.

There in the dark of space, in the space between stars and blocking the stars, the darkness that is growing, roiling like a menacing entity waiting to pounce. One glance at Ikthiel tells me what I already recognize. More careful assessment forces me to realize that they are not beyond the Edge, not outside our universe. These are real. Whatever they are, they are real. And they are inside our universe.

Through Altair's hand I feel a lightning shot of fear and recognition. He says a word, not an English word and not one the translator immediately understands: "Kolvat." Lagging behind the word, the translator simply says "Outsiders."

"We need to get out of here now."

I'm not sure if I said it or Altair or Ikthiel or all three of us. The Witch helps Qidan to his feet. The other Witches stand in a cluster near us.

The Kolvat begin to sink toward the planet now, thick dark tendrils weaving towards us. The darkness blots out what little light is left from the stars, reflecting the light of the fires back at us. Reflecting my own light back at me. My shield so large right now due to the extra power, I feel the eating away of reality at the edges of my perception.

"What are they?" Qidan asks.

Altair responds, "They are from outside the universe. They destroy reality, eat power and matter and energy."

As one, seven Witches look at me. Only Ikthiel remains looking upward.

Qidan asks, "Is there a way to defend against them?"

Altair stares into the overarching dark and shakes his head. "We pushed them out, back out of our universe. But we don't have enough Witches to do that here. Not today and not against so many."

With his words the ground gives a violent shake. Qidan falls and so do several others. Ikthiel grabs my arm and keeps me on my feet. He seems unperturbed by the earthquake. His claws dig into my skin. I feel him tugging at my power. At that moment I don't care. I pour my power into him as well, giving him a sample of what he needs. Surprise lights his face as he pulls back and lets go of my arm.

"Altair, can you transport all of us?" Qidan asks.

Desperation fills Altair's features as I hear and feel him doing the math in his head. I squeeze his hand, reminding him of the power I have been giving to him for probably almost an hour now. In my mind I hear him ask, *Are you sure?*

"Today is not my sparkpoint," I whisper.

The ground shakes again, this time knocking me to my knees. My hand feels glued to Altair's. I look around and see the valley below us the panic setting in. The Reetur's forces run for cover. There in the ground the Kolvat have made contact, a thick shaft of other-matter and other-energy plunges into the ground. The feeding tube to the multitude of beasts in space above us breaks the surface and begins to devour J'Phonk. Horrifyingly I can hear a screeching cry coming from below us, something not heard with the ears but in the heart. The planet is dying.

A shudder runs through me. Forcefully I climb to my feet.

Qidan says, "We have to go now. We can't wait."

Altair turns to me, fear and pain in his eyes as he says, "Give me everything you've got."

"Don't forget the dead," is all I can think to say.

The boundary between us vanishes. The power barrier between all Witches, while necessary at times and easy to circumvent, falls so suddenly I see Altair's deepest memories as if they are my own. Surprise flits through him as he sees my memories as well, every moment with my parents, with my brother, with Ikthiel. Every fear and worry and pain.

Then I let my power go to him.

Altair's mind darts through the list of people we took with us, seeking them out in the dead around us. For the first time, the method he uses to frame his complex jumps becomes crystal clear. I see him choosing to simplify and take all Witches, despite some of the Reetur's forces still falling into that category. By focusing on the Witch's Spark, he gathers everyone into his reach, even Ikthiel.

The demon's hand falls on my shoulder again, easing the mode of transit.

From above, the Kolvat tendrils make their way down toward us. I find it difficult to look at them. Determinedly, I face upward and let my eyes go over the roiling mass of inky night. The revulsion creeps into me as it did at the Edge.

Above us, maybe a few hundred feet over our heads, the tendrils stop. The Kolvat pause. By now my power has saturated Altair so much he will enact the jump at any second. The screams of the dying inundate the air. For some reason I am still staring at the paused tendrils of the Kolvat above us.

A tiny line of other-energy snakes down to us, stops at it hits the bubble of my power saturating me and Altair. From the singular connection, I feel the creatures consider us, weighing the power and desiring to consume it.

"*WE SEE YOU.*"

Ice fills my soul. My stomach drops.

"Now," I whisper. "Get us out *now.*"

My power jerks in Altair's direction, feeding even more into the jump. My shield holding back the Kolvat vanishes in that tug. The Kolvat tendrils dive towards us, rapidly closing the distance. A crushing weight of incomprehensible darkness falls from the sky.

Fear paralyzes me. We won't survive this. I can't breathe.

Then we are on Unosa.

Altair has jumped all of us all the way back.

My heart races within me, the adrenaline still coursing unrestricted. I can't get the sight of the Kolvat sinking towards us out of my mind.

Altair lets go of my hand, breaking the power flow.

My legs go out from under me and for a moment I think I might pass out. Ikthiel's hand still grips my shoulder. He grabs me around my waist and keeps me from falling over. Altair, realizing his mistake, takes my other arm. Slowly, they help me sink to the ground and rest my head on the floor. I know we are in the hanger on the base on Unosa. I know we are surrounded by the dead and the survivors, both allies and enemies. All I can focus on is my pounding heart and the fear at the memory of the Kolvat.

It will take a while before the flurry of activity reaches us in the middle. The many Witches—medics and otherwise—who stayed behind on Unosa, move forward to assess the survivors. I can't seem to move.

Altair rubs my shoulder in concern. I feel Ikthiel sweeping a healing hand over my back, no longer concerned about who can see it. He finds no injuries.

"It's alright Penny," Altair whispers. "We're safe here."

I shake my head, my forehead still against the floor. "No, we're not."

"One problem at a time," Ikthiel whispers. "Just one at a time."

"Breathe."

Closing my eyes, I take Altair's suggestion. Processing what I have just seen will take a long time. The terror I felt will take a long time to shake.

"Is the Powerhouse injured?" I hear a voice ask.

"Don't call me that," I grumble, my voice muted by the ground.

"Uninjured," Ikthiel reports. "Shaken, but uninjured."

I hear the medic tapping on his portable console before saying, "Take her to room seven-oh-six. Just down the hall. She can rest there."

Altair gently takes my right arm, Ikthiel my left. I slowly lift my head from the cool floor. Around me the direness of our situation hits home. As far as I can count, the only Witches to make it off J'Phonk alive are the Reetur's forces and the half dozen with Qidan.

Not for the first time I wish I could be a child again, oblivious to the suffering around me. I close my eyes and let them take me across the room.

I cannot shut out the screams.

22

*NOW*

At some point when I am sitting in room 706, Ikthiel hands me a cup of hot chocolate. A genuine cup of hot chocolate. In a mug that reads "World's Best Dad." I wonder whose kitchen he conjured that from.

I look up at him from where I am sitting curled up in a ball. My fear has abated some, but my hands tremble just holding the mug. I feel weak and my fear at feeling that in front of him must show in my eyes. He sits down next to me. This odd piece of furniture resembles a daybed. I lean my shoulder into his.

Across this small room, Altair sits on another daybed thing, his knees drawn up and his face down. From his memories, I know the last time he used anything close to that much power was when he left his homeworld. His parent's power moved him last time.

It's an odd thought that crosses my mind. He can use a huge amount of power to move one person a long distance, or he can use the power to move a lot of people a shorter distance. The limits on his abilities seem to shrink regularly.

As they do on mine.

Halfway through the hot chocolate I find my voice again.

"What do we do now?" I croak out.

Altair pulls his head up and rests his chin on his knees. "We go back to Widdershin."

Silence meets his words. We all know we have to go home. But what we saw was not going to go away.

"They know who we are," I whisper.

I hold Altair's gaze for a long moment. I can see the fear in his eyes. Knowing him as I do now, I can feel him going through the possibilities in his mind over and over. How much can the Kolvat know? He was on the team that pushed the Kolvat out of his home universe. He was young then, younger than I was when I first discovered my power. As we look at each other I remember his memories, just as he is probably doing now.

"Where are they from?"

"We never found out."

"If they've broken through, we don't have much time," Ikthiel says.

Out of the corner of my eye, I see his features set with worry. I feel it through his contact with my shoulder.

I down the last of my hot chocolate and hand the mug to Ikthiel. It disappears, I assume back to whatever kitchen he took it from.

"What do they want?" I ask no one in particular. "And does anyone know anything about them?"

Ikthiel stands up. "I should consult with my colleagues," he says. "I don't know if they know anything, but I will find out."

For a moment I don't say anything, but then I ask, "Did I give you enough?"

He shakes his head. "But enough for now."

Altair looks at me questioningly, but I don't explain. We all stand up now, purpose filling us again.

"Back to Widdershin," Altair says to me. To Ikthiel he asks, "What if we need you there?"

The demon gives his most demonic grin. "I will find a way through."

I feel a smirk come onto my face. My old rule-breaking demon friend. Even that bit of amusement can't break through the depths of anger and fear in me.

"You're going now?"

"Yes," he says. "I'll meet you soon."

For a second he squeezes my hand, his thoughts telling me he isn't lying and that he does need what he asked. Then he lets go and he is gone.

Altair opens the door to the busy hallway. Our walls, opaque while the door was shut, go transparent. Madness fills the corridor. I see too many people going past.

"What's going on?" I ask.

He shakes his head. "Let's go," Altair says. He's not rude enough to transport within an interior room like Ikthiel does. He typically says his goodbyes first.

In the middle of the chaotic hanger, we find Qidan surrounded by a small team. He is perched on a tall stool and looks much further from death than he did back on J'Phonk. When he sees us, his attention completely focuses on us.

"Where is Ikthiel?" he asks.

"Gone for intelligence," Altair says as we approach. "We don't know enough about the Kolvat."

Qidan seems to consider for a moment. He is about to speak when an aide hands him an electronic tablet. He reads the contents and goes pale. "Unosa is evacuating," he explains. "The Kolvat will be here within the hour. Further, we are getting reports from all over the universe of sightings and attacks."

He looks up and makes eye contact with me. "Velnu's primary was just swallowed by the Kolvat."

I feel the floor drop out from under me.

"Nahnu-beit?" I ask.

He shakes his head. "They've been alerted as have all locations touched by your power." His eyes look at Altair, "And yours."

I don't have to look at Altair to know the dread coursing through him.

"Widdershin," I say. "We're going back to Widdershin."

Qidan nods. "I agree that is the best move. They will need you there." He taps the tablet a few times in front of him and both Altair and my wrist communicators light up with copies of his report. "Take that to Widdershin's Head Witch," he says.

"Go now. We can evacuate without you," he says to Altair before he can protest. "Get there before the Kolvat do."

Altair clamps his mouth shut. There's a pause when he seems to be arguing with himself. Then he cups his hands together and I watch as he manifests the complex teleportation spell matrix he gives out like candy to anyone who needs one. This one, however, is vastly more intricate than the simple sphere I keep in the back of my mind. When he hands the matrix to Qidan, it is the size of a soccer ball, with so many lines it seems like a solid surface.

Qidan takes the matrix carefully, his eyes wide as he studies it.

"Get as many people in one place as you can. The matrix will do the work for you." He looks around the hanger. "It'll move the ships as well."

The look Qidan gives Altair is a mixture of respect and awe. He gives a nod of approval before saying, "Go."

Without pausing for breath, Altair clamps his hand around mine and we are gone in the next moment.

# INTERLUDE

Kaldreesa feels the tremor of earthquakes so regularly they rarely wake Imfra-Rega. She doesn't think it's the tremor that woke her. The swaying of the ceiling is nothing new, but she can't think what would have pulled her out of her deepest sleep. One glance across the home tells her the children are still sleeping. Part of her feels odd knowing that Altair is not there, hidden between her children's more sizable bodies.

Imfra-Rega leaves her youngest children and steps out from under the awning. The neighbor's house is a long distance to the west of them, but even from here Imfra-Rega's sharp eyes can see that she is not the only one to emerge from their home. The peace of the night is disturbed.

She does not know what caused the tremor. The ground is still, even now. For a moment she dismisses it as a passing quake, something Kaldrasticans have gotten used to eons ago.

Then the earth shudders again.

From behind her the children come out of their home and join her on the plateau.

One of them asks, whispering, "What is that?"

Imfra-Rega follows the child's gaze upward, to the darkness filling the sky. Only now does she realize that the sky is void of stars. Only now does she see the roiling mass of dark shapes filling their sight from horizon to horizon—shapes blotting out the clear night sky.

Her hearts fill with dread as the reality becomes apparent. Slowly she wraps each child in an arm. She has held so many children close in comfort, some not her own blood or species. But here and now she is grateful at least that some of them are far away. Some of them are not here.

A moment later the screams begin. Even from up here she can hear the voices in the valley. Imfra-Rega watches unable to do anything as the ground opens up below and the earth begins to burn.

At long last, after so much time, Kaldreesa dies tonight.

She turns her gaze from the burning land and watches only her children. Grateful her life-mate is gone from the planet, she holds her children.

Almost reflexively she whispers, "We hold you safely."

Around them, their world ends in fire.

# PART 3

23

***BEFORE***

"All right, Penny. Try again," Harilsen says again in that neutral voice of his. I can never tell if he is approving or disapproving.

This field is empty except for half a dozen boulders strewn around it. Each boulder probably weighs more than a car. Harilsen, Ikthiel, and Altair all stand nearby, though at enough of a distance that I have space to mess up. I've known for three months now that I am a Witch and the idea is still new and a bit scary. My birthday was last week and it seemed as good a time as any to finally express my power.

I'm upset that this is still blocked in some way. I can't seem to find the connection with the power like I did when I first saw Ikthiel. I think that is why they brought the demon here.

I glance at him now and he looks human. So does Harilsen though he shouldn't.

They have told me the most basic use of pure power involves moving things with your mind. With the amount of power they think I have, I am supposed to be able to move one of these boulders. I don't understand this. In gym they teach us to work up to heavy things when lifting. Apparently this doesn't work that way.

Again I concentrate on the boulder in front of me and again it remains immoveable. Again I try and again I fail. Was this just a fluke that I could see the demon claws the first time? Am I losing my mind?

"Take a break," Harilsen says.

Everyone relaxes and I see Altair turn to Harilsen for a moment. The demon approaches. I feel I should be avoiding him, but I am not scared of him. He stops a couple feet from me gauging my reaction to him.

"Do you see me for what I am Penelope?"

I will never understand why people insist upon using my full name. I never liked it and always preferred Penny.

"No," I answer.

He steps closer and nods, thinking it looks like. "I am wondering," he says, "what happened the day you saw me. What were you feeling?"

I shrug. "I was just walking home from school and taking my normal shortcut," I say. It's true. I felt completely at ease.

"Relaxed," he says.

I nod, wondering where he is going.

"Perhaps you should try to relax when you move the boulder," he says. "Power does not like to be forced."

"You mean, just relax and think about it moving?" I ask.

He shrugs. "Maybe picture yourself leaning into it, as if you're relaxing next to the boulder," he says.

I think it's ridiculous. I think it's a stupid idea. But at this point I don't have a lot to lose. Nothing else has been working.

"I'll try," I say.

"Good," is all he says before turning back to join the others.

"Ready, Penny?" Harilson asks.

I shake off the odd feeling I have talking to the demon. He's not normal and it doesn't feel normal to talk to him. I'm not used to him yet I think.

"Ready," I say.

"Give it a try."

I look at the boulder in front of me and realize how hard I am staring at it, how hard I am concentrating. I take a deep breath to steady myself and relax. Instead of concentrating on the boulder, I just casually look at it. Kinda lazily look at it, as if

I have better things to do. Which, to be honest, if I can't do this then I will have better things to do.

What was it Ikthiel said? Lean into as if I'm just standing next to it?

Sure, why not?

So I think about standing next to it and leaning a shoulder into it like I do at school when waiting in line. Or like I do in the kitchen when watching my mom make cookies. Just relaxed and casual like nothing is wrong.

The boulder shifts.

I take a sharp breath. It stopped moving the moment I paid more attention to it. So I ignore it again. Ignore the feel of the stone and the rocks and everything else around me, glancing around and casually counting every boulder. There are seven of them. Three are particularly big.

Then I mentally lean into the boulder again. I mentally feel myself with gentle hands picking up the boulder and lazily holding it.

All seven boulders lift ten feet off the ground.

"Holy—," I hear Altair say.

After a moment I feel the strain in my mind. Mentally I drop the boulders to the ground again. With a thud that shakes the ground under me, they hit the earth in this windless field in the middle of nowhere.

I immediately sit down, panting like I've just done several sprints in gym class. I was never athletic and this is the first time I regretted that.

Harilsen, Ikthiel, and Altair walk over to me. I look up at them, squinting in the sunlight.

"Was that good?" I ask.

Ikthiel extends a hand to me. Only it's not just a hand. It's a hand ending with claws at the end of each finger. Black claws that come straight from the finger and curl over. Must be murder to push any buttons.

Cautiously I take his hand and stand up. I don't let go for a moment and touch the claws. Then I let the hand drop and look up to find him smiling at me. The smile is disturbing.

Harilsen is not just the human semblance that hides the real person underneath. I can see the alien whose form I've only seen once before. I can see it now. I can see through it now.

"Most practiced Witches would have trouble lifting one boulder, Penny," Harilsen explains. "That is very good."

"What did you do?" Altair asks.

"I relaxed," I say. I look over at the nearest boulder, think about only that one without focusing. I take a breath to calm down, then casually lean into it with my mind.

The boulder rolls fifteen feet away from us.

"You relaxed," Altair says, shaking his head. He's only thirteen, but he seems so much older than me. He is so well practiced with his power.

"If it works," Harilsen says without finishing the thought. "It was enough to get a sense of your scope. We will revisit again later."

Everyone nods, including me.

"We'll have Altair pick you up after school in two days," Harilson says consulting what I swear is a fancy smartphone. "Does that work for everyone?"

I nod, knowing I have nothing to do.

"Good," he says. He looks at me. "As usual, don't show your abilities, discretion is a must. I'm not sure even your family would be ok with it."

When they talked to my family a few weeks ago, the tension in the room was palpable. Harilsen, Altair, and a woman named Alicia Cole were there. I didn't get the sense that my parents were open-minded about the whole thing, but I feel like they are in shock. I think they'll come around if they have enough time. It was a shock to them that species other than humans exist.

"Altair, would you take Penny home?" Harilsen asks.

"Yes," he says. He offers his hand to me. I take it and we are gone from that empty field.

Altair places me in a stand of trees near my house. We are shielded from view as we appear from nowhere. He lets go of my hand.

I am about to walk away when he says, "Wait."

I turn and look at him expectantly.

"Did Ikthiel tell you about the relaxing thing?" he asks.

I nod in reply. "It helped."

"It does, but be careful," he says warningly. "You might start moving things without meaning to. Harilsen didn't say it, but your power was off the charts. We have no idea how strong you actually are."

I feel the surprise on my face, but I don't really understand what that means. "So what should I do?"

"Learn to use brute force," Altair says. "And be careful."

"Ok," I answer. Altair has never given me a reason to doubt him.

"I'll pick you up in two days," he says.

"Bye," I say as I walk out of the trees. I feel him disappear behind me and marvel that I felt it at all.

The world is different now.

24



I blink and the quad comes into focus around me.

The serenity of Widdershin envelops us. In the sky above us, the twinkling lights of the galaxy just begin to become visible as the sun sets in the distance. Witches stream in and out of buildings going about their normal lives. My heart squeezes in my chest feeling a sense of responsibility at disrupting that normalcy. I feel almost a sense of panic at needing to warn them.

Altair tugs at my hand, then lets it go as he starts jogging across the quad. I sprint to catch up to him. Together we go through one of the enormous doors of the main scholarship and administrative building. I even have a tiny study in this building, a room I feel a sudden longing for as I realize how much is at stake here.

Altair leads us past the reception hall and the curious but otherwise unalarmed staff still there. Someone staffs the reception point at all hours of the day. We head into an elevator like the one in Firrl's research lab and Altair pushes the button. The elevator begins to move. Altair and I stand in stony silence waiting.

The elevator doors open to the top floor. While the ceilings are significantly taller and the hall wider than any human corporate office, in all other respects this could be a high-rise office building on Earth. A wide conference-type room sits across the hall, glass acting as a wall between the elevators and that space. There is no table in there, by that is not unexpected with the variety of species working on Widdershin.

Altair leads me to the right and down a carpeted hallway complete with images of past Head Witches and the occasional plant. At the end of the hall, he takes a right into a side corridor that opens to a lush reception area, a single secretary standing behind multiple transparent screens with a variety of data going across them.

"We need to see Head Witch Kelar Zyneste," Altair says without prelude. "It's an urgent emergency communication."

The secretary, another Granician like the one I had worked with on Nahnu-beit, steps out from behind the screens and studies Altair and myself. I don't know how much remnants of the fray on J'Phonk still cling to us, but whatever they see must convince them we are serious. Somehow I doubt they would take two teenagers as seriously as they're taking us now.

The Granician sprouts extra legs and moves to the other door, gently opening it while we stand there. They step through and a murmured conversation ceases followed by the Granician's sliding voice explaining the situation. Then the door opens fully and Altair and I are waved through.

About a dozen individuals populate the room, some sitting in chairs or on racks or benches and some simply standing. Each has a tablet or holographic display in front of them that they look up from as we come in. Altair walks directly to the center of the room and looks at the tiny alien dwarfed by the lush chair at the head of the group. I stay close to him, standing next to his right shoulder.

"Head Witch, I apologize for the interruption," Altair begins. "We have a report from Qidan Durmark and we have grave news from the Marquis Delta Belt."

The small alien, a six-armed, four-legged female humanoid with bluish skin, waves for Altair to continue. He taps his wrist communicator and sends Qidan's report to every tablet in the room. Not having read the report yet, I am not sure what they can be seeing. Their reaction tells me Qidan did not pull any punches.

"*What can do this to a planet?*" an Aix at one side of the room says, their thought-voice filled with horror.

"In my universe, we called them the Kolvat," Altair says.

To my right, a Feirlu using an electromagnet as a resting place says, "Qidan's details are sparse. You can expand?"

Altair nods. "They came into my home universe, but not nearly as many as this. I was part of the team that pushed them back out," he says. "My affinity for teleportation makes moving large objects possible, as you know. In my universe, it took a galaxy's worth of Witches to move them." A murmur runs through the room as these most senior Witches consider the ramifications of what he just said. "The physics here are similar to my home universe. They seem to disobey those laws as if they have never heard of such things."

"What do they want?" another voice asks.

"We never found out," Altair says. "We don't know if it's instinct or maliciousness."

"Malice," I say without thinking.

The Witches turn their attention to me.

"How do you know that?" Head Witch Kelar Zyneste asks. She doesn't seem upset or doubtful, just curious.

"I saw them at the Edge, on the other side of reality," I say. "I heard them on J'Phonk." Cold touches my soul thinking of that collective voice and those many moving parts. "I don't know what they want, but they are not friendly."

Silence meets my words. For a moment I wonder if I overstepped when speaking out. Then Head Witch Kelar says to Altair, "What was the solution?"

Altair draws a tight breath. "We trapped them using what we called a void ring, a vacuum of power and energy. Then using a spell matrix I developed, myself and several other teleportation Witches moved them back outside the universe," he explains.

The Witches all eye each other.

"Was the void ring a spell?" Kelar asks.

"No," Altair answers. "It was a single Witch's talent fueled by half the Witches on the team."

The unease in the room is palpable. Unless I am unaware, there is no such Witch in our universe.

"Is this Witch still alive?"

"No. She died in the effort."

Another murmur circulates. Altair and I exchange a glance. The direness of our situation does not escape one Witch in the room. From Altair's eyes, I can see he is genuinely afraid. This is not a threat he expected to see again. And this is not a threat he feels we can combat on our own.

The Witches around us begin to discuss options. Since we have not been dismissed, Altair and I simply wait in the middle of the room to answer questions as necessary. I turn to him and whisper, "What if there's too many to get back out?"

Fear pales his face. "I don't know," he says. "We can contact my people, but I doubt we'll have enough time for that."

I remember years ago learning that despite his teleportation taking only a few heartbeats to jump him from one universe to another, communication is drastically different. It could take months to get a reply from his people.

Behind us the door opens and the Granician secretary comes through, not bothering to shut it. They walk directly to Head Witch Kelar, leaning over to speak to her quietly. Head Witch Kelar's face turns grave. Slowly she stands, the room going quiet at the expression on her face.

"Fellow Witches, I've just received word our major outposts are under attack all across the universe," she says.

The room goes deathly quiet. Then the Witches jump into action, moving around the room quickly. As if they have orchestrated this many times, these highest ranking Witches pull up screens and holographic maps, bringing in data from all over the universe. Finally amidst the images and data all written in the tidy, universal font the Witches use, a three-dimensional map comes up right in front of us. Altair and I back up in unison.

"Pull up the list of worlds," Head Witch Kelar says. The map shifts to bring several worlds into focus right in front of us and lists the status of those worlds under siege. I recognize too many names. So many of them I have worked at, including Velnu from what feels like so long ago. Panicked I scan the list to look for Nahnu-beit, my eyes going through the worlds to try to find the tiny haven.

Then Altair steps forward, transfixed by one image, one name, in the list.

Kaldreesa.

I feel the air suck out of my lungs as I stare at the status bar and the current state of the planet: DESTROYED.

The word sears into my eyes. Altair freezes next to me, his brain not quite comprehending, I think. My mind races to find words of comfort, but I cannot find any. Altair is visibly shaken and I cannot find the words. I don't know how to offer comfort. I don't know what to do.

Many eyes in the room all fix on Altair's shocked face. I wonder how many know his story.

Abruptly he walks out of the room, the silence of the Witches following him.

I follow Altair into the hall. I find him around the corner, his head slumped into his hands. This is the second time his home has been destroyed, his family lost.

Choosing not to overthink it, I reach for Altair and place a hand on his arm. He doesn't shrug me off as I might have done. Instead he turns to me, his face filled with desperation and pain and disconnect. Reality doesn't seem real to him. I can feel the pain in his heart.

"They're gone," he whispers.

"I know," I say softly, as gently as I know how.

He leans against the wall and slumps to the carpet. I kneel next to him, thinking of Kaldreesa and the people there. The feel of Imfra-Rega's arms around me haunts me. I lay an arm across Altair's shoulders and awkwardly try to comfort him. Altair is sobbing now, quietly as if being loud would make it more real. His hands clutch his face like he is holding himself together, trying to keep from falling apart.

I don't know how long we sit like that. The space before me blurs and focuses many times. The hallway with its oddly corporate look blinking in and out of view as I stand there absorbing what has happened. I don't know how to cry over losses like this. I don't know how to feel. Witches come in and out of Kelar's office and leave us alone to mourn. We are teenagers. They give us space to feel, making a wide berth as they walk back and forth to deal with the crisis.

Then I realize what—or who—is walking towards me.

Ikthiel.

The light comes back on inside me. I don't even think about it. I get up and walk briskly up to him and wrap him in an awkward hug. I don't care. Things are so bad I don't care who sees and who knows.

"I heard about Kaldreesa," he whispers. "And Velnu."

"Is it what I think it is?" I whisper back at him.

"Yes," he says, answering my mind's question. "You are the target. You and Altair. Your powers are the target."

I pull back from Ikthiel and look him over. My hands on his shoulders pick up the lack of my power in him and the emotional exhaustion he feels. From the flashes in his mind, I can see the difficulties he faced with his colleagues.

"We have work to do," I whisper, "but make sure you find me. I will help you. I promise."

Ikthiel nods. "I will," he says. "But now we need to raise the alarm here. On Widdershin."

Altair looks up, looks at us as we stand still embracing. His eyes finally focus. "They're coming here," he says. It's not a question.

"Yes."

He gets up. He wipes his face. "Let's tell them," Altair says. Without another word, he rounds the corner and heads into Kelar's office, Ikthiel and I hurrying to keep up.

The room goes completely silent when Ikthiel steps in. All eyes go to us as if a magnet is drawn to the demon.

"How did you get through the defenses?" the Feirlu asks, suspicion in their voice.

"*Does that matter?*" Altair hisses. The anger comes out unexpectedly. I feel the Feirlu recoil.

"Raise the defenses," Ikthiel says. His words point only at Head Witch Kelar who looks at him with intense scrutiny. "The Kolvat will be here before long."

Head Witch Kelar looks at Altair and looks at me. "Can you both vouch for Ikthiel?"

"Yes," Altair says.

"Without hesitation," I add.

The tiny Witch's eyes fall on me and then on my hand on Ikthiel's hand. I maintained contact to keep in his thoughts, but it must look completely different to them. For a moment, there is a pause. Then she seems to shake off her concerns, all of them.

"Raise the shield," she says.

A flurry of activity meets her words and I see in the corner a diagram come up with Widdershin front and center. Around it, the geodesic sphere of power that surrounds the planet goes from typical lower power to full, blinding energy.

Within seconds of the shield going up, the display lights up with contacts all around Widdershin. A collective breath circulates the room.

"They're here."

Head Witch Kelar says, "Open Planetary Defense Control. If they aren't already there, get them there."

Several Witches head out of the room. Belatedly I realize Altair has followed them out.

"Where are you going?" I ask, catching up with Ikthiel still attached to me.

"I need to see them," Altair says. "And PDC is across the quad."

The three of us and several Witches of various shapes and sizes pile into an elevator heading to the ground floor. I barely notice the looks I'm getting for still gripping Ikthiel's hand like it belongs to me. He glances at me in amusement, a silent commentary on my very human self-consciousness.

As we head out of the elevator and down the hall, I remember to close my jacket. It isn't nearly thick enough for the winter still gripping this part of Widdershin. At least it's not snowing.

Abruptly Altair stops in his tracks some twenty feet from the building, the other Witches running ahead of us. Ikthiel keeps me upright as I come to a halt. The wind slices through my jacket, sending a shiver up my spine.

Altair says a word that sounds like a swear.

I look at him and then follow his gaze upward.

An Earth-centric swear comes out of my mouth.

The Kolvat.

25

*NOW*

Widdershin's incredible, complex, enormous shield surrounds it in space. The orbit puts it roughly the same distance as the Moon from Earth. Most Witches barely feel it as they come through. That barrier prevents Ikthiel from teleporting right to the surface. In space, pressed up against that barrier and blotting out the light of the galaxy, the Kolvat eat away at the shield.

My heart starts racing immediately.

"How are they here already?"

"I don't think they follow the laws of physics here. They didn't in my universe."

There is a pause. Then Ikthiel says, "Let's go."

Together we run across the quad following the more senior Witches. The cold slices into my soul, but running helps. By the time we fly through the door, I'm panting from the exertion. I realize then I'm still holding Ikthiel's hand as we head up the stairwell, some three flights behind the nearest Witches. Altair sets a brutal pace, unyielding now that an emergency has been declared.

On the top floor of the building, I finally catch my breath as Altair leads us into the control center. No windows bring light into the place. Floating screens fill the room and each of the Witches from Kelar's office has already taken a place in front of one.

Ikthiel and I follow Altair to a familiar face. Alicia Cole looks us over as we come closer. Like the Witches in Kelar's office, I can sense the concern and confusion at Ikthiel's presence on Widdershin, but she says nothing. We all still look like crap from our time on J'Phonk.

Without prelude, Alicia Cole says, "Penelope, go to the power team and give them a hand." She points in the direction of a group in the corner, several alien eyes studying us at the sound of their team name. "Take Ikthiel," she adds. "Altair, come with me."

Altair doesn't even spare a glance at either of us before following Alicia Cole. I hurry hand-in-hand with Ikthiel. His thoughts betray the concern he has for how dire the situation is. I glance at him as we approach the team, our grim expressions matching.

"Where do you need us?" I ask the first Witch I come to. I don't know their species and the best I can describe them as is reptilian. They glance over their shoulder at the Aix I recognize from the Head Witch's office.

"*Here*," they say, a single semi-corporeal tendril indicated a panel with a blinking power input circle. "*Both of you can connect here—if you choose, Ikthiel*," they add.

We round a center stand of floating holographic screens and step up to the power input. Only now do I let go of his hand, his thoughts receding but not completely gone. Two circles split from the one and Ikthiel and I each place a hand in one. The input node gives way like water, my hand sinking in until it meets resistance and stops. My power flows into the node, monopolizing a lot of my senses with the flow.

Through the connection I can distantly feel the complex spell matrix at the core of the shield. No single Witch could handle direct contact with a matrix so complex. So the contact is muted, buffered somehow to allow input without burnout.

I flood my power through the gate and feel the shield flare. At the edges of my perceptions I can sense the Kolvat eating away at the matrix. My power will buy us time but attract them worse. How can we make a void of power when we keep throwing it at the shield?

The question brings Ikthiel's hand to my shoulder and his thoughts fully back into my mind. In his mind's eye I can see his thoughts chasing an idea. If demons warp Witch's power to change the nature of reality, is it possible for a demon to warp a spell matrix in the same way?

"Could that make it an anti-power shield?" I ask aloud.

"It would take a lot of power and more direct contact," Ikthiel says.

"*Are you suggesting corrupting the shield?*" the Aix asks. I realize the entire power team is staring at us. It's common knowledge by now that I work better with demons than other Witches, but it must still be odd to see in action.

"In a sense," Ikthiel says. "I'm suggesting demonizing it in the same way demon's corrupt power."

The Aix pulls up the full diagram of the shield in detail and blows it up for Ikthiel. "*This is a simulation,*" they say. "*The controls in front of you will let you show us what you mean.*"

Ikthiel's free hand reaches for the control panel in front of him. He places a single claw on a loop and changes the simulation. The tone and tenor of the shield change almost immediately. Every line in the diagram deepens to the same red color I associate with Ikthiel's power. And then darkens completely so that the matrix is almost invisible.

I reach my free hand forward and probe the edge of the sphere. My hand bounces back from the spell. Opposite us, each Witch tests it as well. The matrix bounces back at the touch. Ikthiel makes a few more adjustments. The color of the matrix lines go from steady dark red to oscillating between dark and bright. The wavering beams remind me of fluorescent bulbs in my old classroom when they were getting ready to go out. Ikthiel stops and pulls his claw back again.

I reach out to the shield. My hand doesn't even make it to the matrix. One by one I watch each Witch test it, their hand or claw or appendage just sliding away from the shield as if it's coated in molasses.

For a moment no one says anything. Then the Aix turns their gaze across the room where Head Witch Kelar now stands. I did not even sense her come in.

"*Head Witch!*" the Aix calls out with urgency in the thought-voice. "*We need immediate approval for an unorthodox solution!*"

Kelar's head turns to our direction. Her eyes land on Ikthiel and me and flit to the shield matrix. Immediately she approaches the team and gives no more than a nod of the head.

"*The demon Ikthiel proposed tuning the shield to demonic power frequencies,*" the Aix articulates far better than either myself or Ikthiel could have. "*The changes require Ikthiel to have full access to the shield matrix.*"

Only the planetary Head Witch can grant access to the shield. But more than one senior Witch would need to sign off on letting Ikthiel access such a vital spell matrix.

Kelar turns and lifts an arm to the Feirlu from her council. "Brattibrax, we need you," she says.

The name clicks. Brattibrax runs the Academy side of Widdershin. Their name and seal appear on every certificate in my file.

Briefly the Aix runs through the explanation for both high-ranking Witches. The concern, while apparent on Kelar's face, is less so in the mannerisms of the Feirlu's energy form. Nevertheless I get a sense of hesitation and mistrust from Brattibrax. A feeling confirmed when they turns to speak to us.

"I don't trust you, demon," Brattibrax says. They turns to me. "Nor do I trust you, Powerhouse. Having incredible power does *not* make you trustworthy. Only your actions can tell me if I can trust you, and right now your actions say you trust demons before Witches. Your history with us is not much better."

This is probably the first time someone in authority admitted they do not trust me. It takes real effort to keep me from saying something regrettable. I swallow my pride and my indignation. Saying something immature now would only hinder efforts.

"All my reservations aside, I will grant you *escorted* access to the central shield matrix," Brattibrax says to Ikthiel. "If Kelar agrees, then Phytymlym will escort you there," they adds, nodding at the Aix. To me they says, "You will stay here and continue to work, Powerhouse."

"I agree to your terms," Kelar says almost immediately. To Phytymlym she adds, "Go now."

Ikthiel pulls his claw back from the power port. Briefly he squeezes my shoulder as he circles the console to join the Aix on the other side. Phytymlym curls a tendril of energy around Ikthiel's wrist and the pair immediately teleport. Either Phytymlym has teleportation power or they carries a spell matrix to do it with.

With them gone, Kelar and Brattibrax step back from the power team and begin conversing in quiet tones. The reptilian alien I can't name joins me, taking Ikthiel's spot. I plunge my wrist in deeper and wait for further instructions, rueful that I am only useful as a power source.

"Brattibrax is intimidated by you," the reptilian alien whispers. "They doesn't know what to do with you."

I glance at the Witch and mutter, "Story of my life."

An expression that can only be amusement crosses their face before they turns back to the power shunt. All the Witches on this team are powerful, not like my power but remarkable among typical Witches. For half a second I wonder why I am not on this team already, but the answer is obvious: trust.

"Hold," the reptilian Witch says.

I look in confusion across at the two other team members. One hands me a tiny earpiece that clings to my skin when placed behind my ear. Immediately Phytymlym and Ikthiel's voices come through the comm, discussing timing.

"Penelope, go ahead and pull back completely," Ikthiel says.

Gently, I extract my hand from the power node. The shield display dims as my power flow leaves it. I flex my fingers, noticing that the glow of power still permeates my skin. A momentary flutter of nervousness turns my stomach.

*"Penny, when we complete the adjustments, we'll have you power the changes,"* Phytymlym says, *"But I do not want too much power for the Kolvat to feed on. So we'll just dose the shield for now."*

"Understood," is all I can think to say. I feel a tad useless every time I am not needed, even for powering a spell matrix.

My gaze wanders across the room in time to make eye-contact with Altair. He keeps himself composed in this dire situation, but even from across the room, I can see the pain. His eyes betray the unraveling within him.

The shield suddenly turns a dark red, pulsing with its usual golden light intermittently. My focus goes back to the task at hand. Phytymlym calls out adjustments to the team around me, making tiny nuances to the power inputs and the matrix itself. The adjustments are so advanced they go over my head completely. I just wait.

"*It's time Penny,*" Phytymlym calls out.

I set my hand on the node, sinking into the almost-liquid contact point. "How much do you need?" I ask.

There is a pause. Then Ikthiel says, "Feed it slowly, we'll give you a stopping point."

I nod even though I don't think they can see me. Then the door to my power opens and I let it loose in a more controlled manner than I usually do. Several minutes pass before they call for a stopping point. I pull my hand back from the node, my skin quiet this time.

We hold our collective breaths. My focus narrows to just the shield matrix and the slow adjustments Ikthiel makes. Balancing a planetary shield involves much more delicacy than the simulation.

Minutes crawl by and the incursion on the shield does not lessen. Through the comm I can hear Ikthiel and Phytymlym talking as they work to adjust the shield together. The adjustments change the shield subtly. Outside the shield, darkness falls.

After a moment, I realize someone is standing next to me. I assume it's another of the researchers until I look up. Altair glances down at me, taking his gaze from the shield for only a moment. I reach my hand down to his hand and give it a squeeze. The pain in him seethes just below the surface. I let go.

"*It's working,*" Phytymlym says over the comm. "*Just barely.*"

"Enough to buy us some time," the reptilian Witch says

darkly.

In the display in front of us, the dark halo around Widdershin expands, pushing back the Kolvat just a bit further. For the first time in an hour, I feel my shoulders relax slightly.

"*Penny, can you feed some more power in?*" Phytymlym asks.

I connect to the shield again and trickle power into it. A minute or two goes by and Phytymlym calls a halt. I draw my hand back, the power refusing to die down for the moment. One glance at my hand tells me what I know: the power veils my skin again. I clench my fist. Now is not the time.

The room comes back into focus. I hear the team next to us working to coordinate the off-world effort. The Witches sent across the galaxy to protect other outposts have been recalled now that the primary stronghold is at risk. The Academy always felt like a school to me, but really it's the beating heart of Witch culture.

A group of raised voices across the room pulls my attention. Looking over my shoulder, Altair doing the same, I identify the group. The planetary defense team across the way, coordinating the system-wide defenses beyond just the shield, fights to keep calm. Something has them freaked.

In my ear the comm blasts a series of Aix swears across connection. The shield display in front of us has changed. In one place on the matrix, a tiny, sinister orange circle appears. From this place on the matrix, each line around it dims significantly.

"What the—?" I hear Altair whisper.

"What is it?" I ask, my eyes fixed on the growing circle.

"Unidentified element in play," the reptilian Witch says.

All around the room a flurry of activity drowns out calm. Then I catch one word from somewhere, a word I wasn't expecting.

"Reetur."

My soul runs cold at the name. Ringing fills my ears for a moment. The activity of the room does not get through to me.

Then it's as if the veil is lifted and I hear the voice in my comm again.

"*The power is witchlike and demonlike,*" Phytymlym says.

Another circle appears on the shield.

And another.

And another.

My heart slams in my chest and I can barely breathe.

Silence falls in the room. Kelar has called for order.

"It appears the Reeturs have joined forces with the Kolvat," she says, her voice slicing like a knife right through me. "Adjust accordingly."

Immediately the voice of Witches drowns out the silence.

Altair meets my gaze. The panic in his eyes mirrors that in my heart.

I watch the increasing number of orange circles appearing on the shield display, my heart falling apart inside me.

26



"How long is the shield going to hold?"

"With the Reeturs trying to dismantle it? Not long enough."

I see Alicia Cole across the control center speak into her communicator, get frustrated and try again. Altair next to me catches her eye. She walks directly across the room and up to Altair.

"I can't get ahold of Lealla," she says, desperation in her eyes. "I need to be here. Please, get my wife off this planet."

Altair nods his head and immediately vanishes from the room. I think he might be grateful for something to do. I could feel his mind desperately holding together under the strain. And I can understand that.

My mind races around to all the Witches threatened by the shield going down. I feel fear, real fear, for the people here. I do care about these Witches who have given me a home. And now this home is under siege. My mind goes to Firrl and the research that the group has been working on for millennia.

My wrist communicator buzzes. A single message comes through. It's from Firrl.

> **Already evacuating. Focus on what you
> need to do. We will remember your fire.**

Firrl's ability to see the future must be coming in handy. I hope they all make it out.

"Firrl's research building is already evacuating," I say to Alicia Cole. A tiny bit of momentary relief fills her eyes.

"Good, every bit helps," she says. "Too many Witches and not enough time to transport them all."

Right on cue, Altair reappears. "I moved her and her whole building to Deasil," he says, referring to the next planet in the system, one currently on the opposite side of Widdershin's sun. "I'll keep moving people as long as I am able."

"Here," I say, finally able to do something more than fuel a failing shield. I grab his arm and pour power into him. "You'll exhaust yourself if you don't take it."

Alicia Cole watches this with fascination. Then she says to Altair, "Start with the students in the evacuation zones. I doubt the transport squares are working properly anymore."

Again Altair disappears.

On the display the horrible truth becomes apparent. A gaping hole in the shield opens up. I suddenly taste bile in my mouth, remembering what the attack on J'Phonk felt like. I know what is coming next.

The ground shudders. The building sways around us. The room goes eerily quiet in reaction. Not one Witch believed in their souls that the shield could actually fail.

Alicia Cole's eyes widen in shock. I hear her thoughts for the first time.

*We're going to lose Widdershin.*

The ground shudders again. The whole building shakes in response.

"Get to the roof," a voice calls out.

En masse, we move to the roof, Witches all confident they can fly from the roof faster than escaping from the doors below. A crush of bodies in the stairwell and then open sky as we make it to the roof. Only the sky is not open. The Kolvat shroud the planet, encroaching on the light.

My heart drops into my stomach. There are so many, and the shield has already started to buckle. I can see the glow of Reetur Witch power eating away at spots in the shield. And some of those spots are already breached, a tendril of the Kolvat pushing down and through. They've already made contact with the ground.

Of course they have. I knew that and I shake off my feeling of stupidity for thinking otherwise. It is just so unbelievable and horrifying to see it happening again. Who are the Kolvat? Why are they doing this? Is it instinct? Is it malice?

Again no answers come. Maybe those answers don't matter.

The building shakes beneath me, knocking me to my knees. Around me the Witches lift off the roof and fly from the danger. I can't fly. I can barely levitate under the best of circumstances.

Anger creeps in me. Ridiculously powerful and talented—in ways that really don't matter.

I try to stand up and think about everything Harilsen and Altair and even Ikthiel tried to teach me about flying. I try to defy gravity just one time. The building crumbles around me.

I give up.

I close my fist and think about the spell matrix I use to employ Altair's power. And before I can enact it, I am sitting on the ground in the quad. In front of me and past the landing Witches, I watch the building implode. Horror washes through me. Silently I hope all the Witches inside made it out.

Slowly I climb to my feet. The cold cuts through me, freezing winter complicating the emergency. The Kolvat fill the sky from horizon to horizon, the shield puckering where the Reeturs break it apart. The complexity of the matrix combined with my power and Ikthiel's demonic influence slows them down, but not enough.

Around me the flurry of Witches ignores me, ignores the teenage human who doesn't have anything helpful to offer— just sheer power and no direction to point it in. So much panic fills the Witches around me. How are we going to get out of this? How are several billion Witches going to get off this planet?

Then a thought crosses my mind as I stand in the midst of the fray and the panic of the Witches. With that thought, a divide forms between me and all those around me. I am suddenly my own island.

*I could stop them.*

Distantly I hear someone calling for full evacuation. Distantly I feel Altair flicking out with dozens of Witches in tow, still employing the power I gave him. But I can feel it happening to me. My hands tingle with unreleased power. Looking at them, the thin veil of power thickens, shrouding them, ready when I am.

Where should I go? I can't do this here. I can't defend the whole planet here.

Below my feet I hear the voice of Widdershin echo up through me. She is pained with the attack by the Kolvat, anguished at the thought of her children dying. The fact that I can understand Widdershin's voice so well makes me wonder how much time I have.

Then the idea comes, or I hear it in Widdershin's mind.

The north pole.

The place is central enough I can cast out my shield through the magnetosphere, protecting the whole planet in one shot. It would take incredible power to defend a whole planet. Incredible power is the one thing I had to offer.

I look around me with the eyes of a Witch knowing their time has come. Everything feels pale and unreal. Alicia Cole barks orders to a flurry of Witches around her. Tiny Kelar Zyneste, the powerful Head Witch for Widdershin, stands in the middle of several Witch teams seemingly organizing the evacuation. Like a captain refusing to abandon her ship, she adamantly refuses to be teleported off-world. And then there's Altair. His physical form barely materializes as he frantically teleports a dozen or more Witches at a time off the planet. His effort will not save them all. He needs more time.

Maybe, just maybe, I can give him enough time to save some if not all. Maybe I can help with that.

In my mind I consider Altair's power. I remember seeing in his mind on J'Phonk and finally understanding how he teleports. The frenetic crowd of Witches around me, still ignoring me for the moment, comes back into focus. For a fraction of a second, Alicia Cole makes eye-contact.

Then I am gone before she can say a word.

Silence envelops me.

The voices of panicked Witches remain far behind me, far south in the frenzy of the quad and the panic of evacuation. Even the sounds of the attack, the crackling of the shield folding under pressure, recedes into memory. Around me only the harsh landscape of the north pole fills my view from horizon to horizon. The polar cap stretches around me, glowing a pale silver under the last shreds of light from above. The inky black of the Kolvat blots out the galaxy normally dominating night sky. Against the dark sky, a thin remnant of the aurora shimmers.

I close my eyes and feel the distant edges of the aurora in my mind. I let myself fall down into the hypnotic sensation of a planetary magnetosphere, feeling the crackling energy of every point in the field. The wind whips up around me. Blistering cold turns harsher, but I don't feel it through the thickening shroud of power around me.

For a moment I stare out at the barren landscape, enjoying this last moment before I make my choice. I barely recognize it when a human suddenly stands there.

Altair.

He is actually wearing a winter coat now. Have I been up here long enough for him to grab a coat? I can't feel the cold, but I'm sure it must be fierce. He spots me to his left and jogs to me, shielding his face from the wind.

"What are you doing?" Altair shouts, his voice cut by the wind.

"What I'm meant to do," I shout back. "What needs to be done." I raise my hand, the hand now covered by power spilling out of me.

Altair's eyes go wide.

"You see?" I ask. "It's time Altair. Get them off this world. Make sure they're safe." I fling my hand at him and a ball of power stronger than anything I have shared with him hits his chest. He staggers back from the impact, his face a mask of shock as the power runs into him. He could teleport the whole planet's population in one shot with that. He will need to.

"Go!" I say. "It's time."

Altair wipes his face with a gloved hand, his cheeks glowing with spillover from my power. "I will remember your fire," he says. And I understand what Firrl was saying. Your fire. Your sparkpoint.

With those words he disappears. I am alone.

I could leave right now and never enact my sparkpoint. I could choose to walk away. The shadowy figure I saw on J'Phonk solidifies in front of me. She looks like my long-dead aunt from this close up. She almost looks like me. I swallow my fear and my pain and I make my final choice.

I choose Death.

I think I chose it a million times without realizing it. The bitter irony of my decisions fills me. My life opens up before me like a million-petal lotus revealing its core. I can't help but wonder what I would have been if I were ordinary. I can't help but wonder if I would have been given more time.

And time is against me now.

Above me, above the planet, above the north pole, the Kolvat approach.

Darkness eats away at the sky, a darkness that is not the natural dark of space but the malicious poisonous ink of hatred seeping in every motion of the Kolvat. Billions—maybe trillions—fill my view from horizon to horizon. No longer does the blinking orange of Widdershin's sun illuminate the sky. Neither does the light touch me nor does the cold invade my space. All elements recede from me, perhaps reacting to the power gathering in my bones.

The ground below me shivers in pain and fear. I feel the heart of the planet reverberating in my body. Waves move through my blood, set in motion by the voice below me.

For a moment I shut my eyes. Tears leak out. What kind of hero cries in the end? What kind of hero weeps in the face of their enemy?

I can delay no longer.

Defiantly I look upward.

I worked so hard to be an adult all this time. Everyday became an exercise in maturity and self-control as much as it was an exercise in magic. Today, the last day, I give up.

I stamp my foot in petulant, fourteen-year-old defiance.

"This is MY PLANET!" I scream.

I don't think they can hear me, but I don't care. For once in my short life, all of my inhibitions fall away like so much dust. I forget about the tears or the dirt in my hair or my strange, disheveled clothes, all the destruction of J'Phonk still clinging to me. I don't care who sees me or where I am or that the cold will get to me eventually.

"I WARN you!" The tears warp my voice. I point my finger at the Kolvat determined to be as intimidating as my mother. "This planet is MINE. You CANNOT have her!"

The darkness pauses.

From somewhere far above me, a tendril of ice reaches out to touch my soul. A single fingerlet of sensation tells me I am being considered, evaluated, pondered. I wait, refusing to so much as flinch in the face of that scrutiny. I hate the evaluations here at the Academy. I hate the judgment and the consideration. But I will not bow my head nor lower an eyebrow for my instructors. Nothing can make me do that for the Kolvat.

The needle thin touch pulls away quicker than it came. I wait.

And then the Kolvat move.

Horrorstruck, I watch the darkness sink towards the planet again.

The Kolvat are not impressed.

An old inner demon from my childhood rears its ugly head. My jaw clenches. My nails bite into my palms as I squeeze my fists. Anger seethes in me at being so easily dismissed. Echoes of my father's angry accusations and my mother's dismissive tone haunt me.

The Spark smolders within me.

I glare at my enemy and feel the rising power within me.

Second after second squeezes past me. I only have a few more before I no longer have a decision to make and nature—or power—will take its course. This power—my power—will enact itself and take my life in balance. To save the life of a planet, the life of a Witch—my life—will be the payment.

The trade seems fair.

Death nods in approval. Her face, my long-dead aunt's face, looks at me with respect.

I feel the power coming now. My Spark finds its purpose.

This is the faith of the Witches. This is their religion. And only now do I fully understand why.

Power like the Hand of God fills me.

And I lift my hands to the heavens and in my soul I begin to pray.

27

## BEFORE

The history book lays spread open in front of me. The chapter on Sacagawea lost my interest thirty minutes ago. Thanksgiving is coming up and my mind is on that and the impending holidays. I always like Christmas.

The clock on the library wall clicks forward. 4:00. Time to go home.

Triumphantly I close the book. I shove my schoolbooks in my bag and pick up the library book. At the front desk, the old librarian checks it out for me and bids me a good evening. I come here almost every day after school, they are so used to seeing me.

Outside the library doors, the afternoon air has turned muggy. It's November but this far south we don't really get fall. The trees all around retain their green and their Spanish moss like the idyllic version of the South people up north imagine. Nobody thinks about the heat that much. Or the humidity.

Rather than go to the nearest intersection to cross the street, I dart across between cars and begin my walk home by going through the Dollar General parking lot. At the back of the lot, I cut through the trees, crossing Market before going through more backyards till I get to our house on Haven. Within a few steps the trees enfold me in their peacefulness, shutting out the light traffic and the stray voice or two from the elementary school playground. Only the brush crunching under my shoes breaks the silence.

"I don't understand."

I freeze. The voice was a whisper. I don't usually see people back here.

Cautiously I edge forward through the trees, uncertain about the kind of people I would find in the woods.

"By these readings, there should be dozens around here." The voice sounds like it belongs to a boy.

Curious, I take a few cautious steps forward and peer around the trees.

A low glow lights up the dimness under the trees. I blink a few times, staring at what I'm seeing. There is a boy, not much older than me, maybe in early high school from his features. But he is tall for someone that age. The man with him is taller, with dark features and a lanky build. They are both dressed oddly, in clothes that don't seem normal, materials that are metallic but fitted well to the body. The colors are muted and only faintly reflect the glow.

That glow. What is that? My eyes fix on the light hanging in the air between them. A web of red and gold lines hovered in the air, blinking and pulsing in a rhythm. The boy reaches for some of the lines and pokes them. The lines brighten.

"I don't understand," he repeats.

The man reaches for the light. My eyes land on his hands. For a moment I don't understand what I'm seeing. Then it clicks.

Each finger ends in a dark, curving cruel claw, the point bending almost back to the finger itself. Each hook looks dark and evil.

A jolt runs through me at the sight of the claws. I drop the library book.

Immediately their eyes fix on me. The boy's eyes surprised or startled, the man-creature's impassive. The lines of light flash once and then blink out. The boy walks slowly over to me, the other one hanging back and keeping his distance.

The boy stops several feet from me but reaches down and picks up the library book. He hands it to me. "Who are you?" he asks.

"Penny," I say, accepting the book and hugging it close to my chest.

"Do you live around here?"

"Yes." My eyes go to the creature with the claws. "What is he? Why does he have claws like that?"

The boy and the creature look at each other, confused. To me the boy says, "You can see his claws?"

"Can't you?"

The boy nods, "Yes."

The man-creature studies his claws for a moment then says to the boy in a surprisingly normal voice, "The illusion is intact. I don't understand."

"Maybe she can see through it?"

The creature approaches and kneels down in front of me. Without thinking, I take a step back. Neither of them stops me. Neither touches me nor tries to keep me there. That alone makes me relax a smidge. I am afraid of the creature, but if they were going to hurt me, wouldn't they be trying to keep me here? And why would the boy trust this creature if he was dangerous?

The creature holds out his clawed hand to me. I look at the boy who seems confused.

"What are you doing?" he asks.

The creature glances up at the boy but says to me, "I want to know if you can feel the claws or only see them."

"Why?" I ask.

"Because if you can only see them, then my illusion has failed," he says. "If you can feel them, then it's something more."

"You mean you think she's a Witch too," the boy says.

A witch?

My confusion must show. The boy only shrugs.

I hesitate. Then I reach out and take the creature's hand as if to shake it. My palm meets heat. The kind of heat felt when reaching out to a fire for a second too long. It isn't exactly uncomfortable.

The creature stares at me with dark eyes, then turns to the boy and says, "You try."

The boy takes my hand next, his eyes going wide in shock. "Is she what we're picking up here?" he asks the creature. To me he says, "How often do you walk through here?"

I shrug. "Almost every day." I take my hand back.

The creature stands up and says, "A latent trail." He says this as if it is some sort of fact he is pronouncing.

The boy nods in agreement. "Not enough of us here on Earth to make this big of an impression," he says. "It's all her."

"What does that mean?" I ask.

"It means you're the person we've been looking for," he says. To the creature he says, "We'll have to let Alicia Cole know and get an assessor out here."

The creature continues to stare at me but nods in vigorous agreement. "Don't wipe her memory," he says. "I don't think she knew she had this before and we might bury it for good."

Slowly, what he said becomes clear. Wipe my memory?

"I agree," the boy says. To me he asks, "Can you keep a secret? Can you keep it secret that you met us? That you saw Ikthiel?"

My eyes go to the creature and down to his claws. "Your name is Ikthiel?" I ask, pronouncing the name carefully.

The creature nods.

"What are you?" I ask. It might be rude to ask.

"Ikthiel is a demon," the boy answers. "I am what some call Witches and others call Guardians or Protectors." The way he says those names makes them seem important. Like they mean something more than what I understand.

"What is your name?"

The boy answers, "Altair Nebeck."

Strange name.

"Altair," I say, trying it out.

I glance at the man-creature, what did he call him? Demon? A chill runs down my spine.

"I'm going home."

The boy nods. Clutching the library book tightly, I turn and hurry through the woods. Over the crunching my feet on leaves and pine needles, I hear the demon say, "What do you make of her?"

"I don't know, but I'm surprised they don't know there's a witch with that much power here."

"Especially since there are so few on Earth."

"We'll have to come back."

I let the sound of my feet drown out their words. I let the afternoon normalcy drown out the thoughts in my mind.

Only my brother is home when I let myself in the backdoor. My mother must be out at church or someplace else. Quietly I make my way up to my room. I drop my backpack by my bed and sit down on the patterned quilt. My eyes roam around my room to the picture of Jesus and the cross on the wall, the few posters I have of the Christian music groups I like and the one poster of my favorite book I got by going to the midnight book release. I pull my knees close to my chest.

Only there in the safety of my room do I let myself think about what just happened, what I just saw. The image of the demon's claws fills my mind, fills every corner of my soul choking me with fear.

Tightly I close my eyes, thinking over and over that I'll never see them again.

28

*NOW*

"Penelope!"

Ikthiel has finally come. I knew he would come. He is almost too late.

Slowly, I lower a hand and hold it in his direction. Power pours from me in a flow I can barely control. It hits the demon full on and wraps him in more power than he or his demon friends could ever use. He staggers backward almost falling in the onslaught. When he regains his balance again, I watch as he walks towards me not stopping till he is a foot from me.

He raises one clawed hand and holds a ball of red demon's power in it. He offers it to me.

"Why?" I ask.

"An exchange," he whispers. "You will need it."

Trusting his ability to see the future, I take the power into my hand and then into me. I feel the ball of power tighten up, shrink down, and settle in my heart. Feeling the steadiness of it there, next to my own Spark, my power feels more controlled. As if the control he has over his power is something available to me now that I hold it.

"You should leave," I say to Ikthiel, glancing over his shoulder at Death. My aunt's face looks sad.

"No," Ikthiel says. "I will wait with you."

185

My eyes meet the demon eyes of my friend. I look into him, into his mind, in ways I had been afraid to until now. In him I see the protectiveness he has felt for me for so many years. In him I see the fearless acceptance of a young Witch as his friend. Because we are friends. Not just for my power.

I reach out and take his hands.

"Thank you for bringing help," I say. I know now that he is the one who kept me from dying on the kitchen floor more than a year ago. "Thank you for watching over me."

Then I let go of his hands and send him away from me. He appears over a mile in the distance. I do not let him teleport back.

My attention returns to the planet beneath my feet and the Kolvat in the sky above me. All around Widdershin, anywhere my current bubble does not touch, the tendrils of the Kolvat dig into the surface of the planet.

In the distance I feel Altair pull off the most spectacular teleport of his life. The power I gave him balloons out and takes every soul living and not off this planet. For a moment the teleport brushes over me, but I am so far gone into my power even Altair cannot move me. Ikthiel disappears and I am alone again.

My hands go up, my palms reaching for the sky. I turn my face upward, the tears falling down and tickling my ears with dampness. I don't care. In my heart I let go of everything. Let go of the human part of me and worldly concerns. All my past is behind me now.

The Spark erupts inside me.

The tiny bead of Ikthiel's demon power flickers, barely a whisper in the face of my Spark. In that tiny flicker I regain some control, my mind directing the power into my shield, into the magnetosphere. My shield shoots out like an arrow into the sky. I feel it run through the magnetic field wrapping around the planet like a protective cocoon.

The Kolvat press against the shield, daring me to fail. My heart stutters with the effort to hold the line. Rather than pull back I push my power out deeper into the shield. My vision blurs then goes dark, but it doesn't matter. I can feel my power pouring out, leaving me to protect Widdershin.

My hands feel cold.

Reality shifts. I can see again, through the veil of the corporeal world this time. The landscape on Widdershin has vanished. I find myself in twilight. All around, the hazy gray of the between spaces. And I am not alone. Two women stand with me. Beyond the circle of the three of us, my eyes fail to focus on anything. If there is anything out there, I cannot see it. I focus on the women.

Before me, the figure with my aunt's face.

"You're Death," I remark, as if that is her name.

She smiles and says in English, "One concept I am called."

"But you look like my aunt."

"Do I?" she says surprised. "I look like whoever is easiest for you."

"Oh."

I look at the other woman. She's made of stone and earth and wood with hair like the ocean and eyes like the clearest sky. But she is old, her hair flowing like the ebbing tide, the rock of her fingers frail and crumbling at the tips. Still I can feel her strength. My eyes run over the color of her hair, the same color of Tethys Bay. I suddenly know who she is.

"Are you Widdershin?"

"That is the name they gave to me," she says, her voice cracking with age.

"What's happening? Am I dead?" I ask.

Death smiles coyly. "You have a choice," she says, amusement in her voice.

"I made my choice."

"This is different. An offer has been made to spare you," Death says indicating Widdershin.

"My choice is to save Widdershin," I say. Calmness has taken over. I'm not afraid of Death or what happens here if I make that choice. I know I have done what I could to save the Witches on Widdershin. I know my choice.

Widdershin comes close to me. "My child," she says, taking my hand in her crumbling stony fingers. "My time has come over and over again. So many of my children have died to save me and save each other. And now you have done what I could not do. You empowered one to save them all."

She raises a hand to brush away the tears flowing freely from my cheeks.

"I don't want to be a demon," I whisper. "I don't want to be like the Reeturs."

"This is not the same as that. This is a willing substitution," Death says.

I look at Death. "Isn't this my time?"

She looks amused. "Who told you there was only one time?"

"It's ok child," Widdershin says. "You can let go."

I close my eyes, letting the tears flow.

When I open them again, Widdershin's barren north pole spans out before me. It felt like a dream. An illusion or a hallucination or something between the two. But also real.

Sobs fill my chest. My power seeps back down into me from the shield. I no longer feel the cold.

"*No.*" The word comes out in a croak, a gasp. Desperation fills me as I feel the planet beginning to crumble under the sway of the Kolvat. I am still here.

As distinctly as I heard the old woman's voice, I hear the deep reverberating voice of the planet under my feet. No words come to my ears. No understanding fills me now.

The ice glows a pale yellow, brightening under my feet. Without warning the energy of the planet herself strikes. A blast of power eclipsing my own pours from the planet's heart beneath me. My soul burns with the power pouring through me, my hands sending more power than I dreamed possible into the sky, into the shield.

I can't hold back the scream. The planet's power competing with my own and the flicker of demon power, twisting my soul around in a mobius strip of incongruity. Nothing makes sense or fits together. The powers are incompatible but somehow this *must* work. The planet is *dying* for this.

My ribs expand forcing in what feels like my last breath. The planet's power flows into me and through me like I am the banks of a raging river. Widdershin's power breathes in every cell of my body. My legs shake with the effort of standing, of holding the shield, of keeping the Kolvat at bay. I am a corridor, a pathway for this power. Maybe this is why I have so much power: so that I can sustain a flow of power like this.

Even I can't sustain this forever. And eventually Widdershin's power will be exhausted. All things end eventually. Maybe that is what they were trying to tell me. Maybe this is not my end after all.

I shake off my rogue thoughts. There has to be a way to make this power do something useful, really useful for the universe. There *must* be a way to stop this.

What did Altair say? What did they do?

They shoved the Kolvat out of the universe into the between space they came from. And it took more Witches than we have and a Witch's power that does not exist in this universe. But maybe I don't need to do that. Maybe I don't need that Witch's power to trap the Kolvat. They are diving headfirst into the planet right now. Maybe I can just open a one-way door out of our universe and let them fall into it.

The heart of the planet. Open a door at the heart of the planet.

From beneath me I hear the garbled voice of Widdershin, a nonsensical series of soul-felt noises that only mean one thing: *yes.*

Even on J'Phonk there was another way. Here I would have to take the planet's life.

I picture a sphere like a door to the other side. In my mind all the details of Altair's teleportation power come back to me. There is not enough time to truly master it, and some Kolvat are sure to escape. Does it really matter if I could get some to disappear?

No spell matrix, just power. A delicate balance. Above: Widdershin's power and Ikthiel's demon power to maintain the lines of the shield. Below: my power casting down to create a portal.

The moment the door opened, I felt it. Not the door. Widdershin's screams.

I start sobbing and I'm not sure I can stop. The pain Widdershin feels, if it can be called pain, courses through me as the last legs of the planet's power leaves. I did this and I can't escape that. No corner of my mind or my soul offers a place to hide.

I lower one hand. The lines of the shield bow out from the planet, bow out as the magnetic field begins to fail. Above me I can just make out the reddish demon power interlacing the yellow glow from Widdershin. Widdershin's last gasp of power flies up through me, the voice of the planet silent now. The yellow fades and I let it go.

The ground crumbles around me. Every inch of Widdershin's core has been replaced with a portal out of our universe. The mantle and the crust begin collapsing into it just as the Kolvat come raining down from the sky. All around me tendrils of their inky black terror hit the ground, eating away at the ice sheet. I lower my second hand and let Ikthiel's power go as well. Nothing stops them now. My mind goes blank at the sight of their darkness blotting out the sky. All I can hear are the remnants of Widdershin's screams.

I know I should teleport out. I just can't remember how. All I see are the Kolvat falling from the sky around me. All I can concentrate on is the feel of the portal eating them, eating the first tendrils as they hit the core.

Something hits me in the chest nearly knocking the wind out of me. My arms collapse around shoulders and I realize I'm holding onto a person. I blink once, twice and Widdershin's collapsing landscape vanishes. The planet hangs in space before me, at enough distance to be out of its gravity well. From here, I look over the shoulder of the person holding me and watch as the Kolvat fall into the trap, into the doorway I have created.

"Breathe, Penelope," Ikthiel says, leaning back to look at me and look at what was a planet only a short time ago.

He places a clawed hand on my chest. Air enters my lungs. I forgot I could breathe. I realize I'm still crying. Sympathy fills the demon's face. He wraps me in his arms and I cry on his shoulder, unabashedly sobbing before the demon.

He starts teleporting, but I don't let him. We hang in space and watch the planet crumble, the Kolvat falling into the trap laid for them. Like the last water down the drain, the doorway sucks them in faster and faster, a few escaping to fly past into the depths of space. I'm not sure how much time passes. I witnessed every last molecule of Widdershin and every Kolvat that could not escape get sucked into that sphere at the heart of what was a planet. Someone should witness the death of a planet. Especially this planet that harbored Witches for so long.

After a moment, a void fills what was our home. I close my eyes and bury my face into Ikthiel's shoulder, letting go of my hold on his power.

I feel the cold of space give way to warmth.

29



*NOW*

The infirmary lights come up a tad as my eyes open. Technically it's the middle of the night, but again I find myself awake. Around me in the patient ward, the main lights stay low. Only the strip on the wall behind my bed comes up.

I don't move. I remember the dream again, the twilight there. The infirmary lights remind me of the twilight between life and death. My eyes focus on the translucent divider between me and the patient next to me. For a moment I see nothing but the face of Widdershin, her old eyes clear as the sky.

No one comes to my side. I look to the foot of my bed and the chair in my area. Ikthiel sleeps there, as peacefully as demons sleep. Every time I wake up, even for a moment, either he or Altair have been there. Once Firrl waited outside my area, her mind brushing over mine when I woke. No one has bothered me. They have all given me space.

After Widdershin fell, it was only a matter of time before Deasil would destabilize as well. The planet's orbit began shifting immediately and the Witches again began evacuations. This time there was not as much of a rush. Every ship willing to carry Witches came. Every portal on Deasil opened and a vast amount of Witches crossed into a constellation of planets around the quadrant. Myself and many wounded Witches were taken aboard a medical cruiser run by another species I had never heard of till that day.

Every night for over a week I had spent less than a few hours asleep at a stretch. The healers in the infirmary come by during the day to feed me and make sure I am still in one piece. The mind-healer told me it would take a while to recover from the psychological shocks I have been through. I don't doubt it. I can barely understand what I have seen.

When I told them what I saw, what I had experienced, it was difficult for them to understand. Whether they didn't believe me or didn't believe it was real, I couldn't be sure. Altair told me later, quietly, that he believed it *was* death personified. Such things happen in his universe regularly, but here the rules might be different. When I asked if he had ever seen death, he didn't answer and that was enough for me.

So much to process, so many things to think about and consider.

I press my hand to my heart and feel the demon power there. I thought it had exhausted itself on Widdershin. I thought it was gone. But there it lives, next to my Spark.

Ikthiel wouldn't take it back either. He said the need was still there. I didn't have the energy to ask more. Whatever he saw that led him to give me the power could not be a problem right now. And my curiosity felt dead. Everything felt unnecessary, like it didn't matter.

Ikthiel stirs in his chair. He opens his eyes and meets mine. He scoots the chair closer to me and pulls my blanket up a little higher on my shoulder.

"Hello," he whispers. He watches me watch him, my mind meeting his and not pushing. I've seen into him now and I know him more than I thought I would. I don't probe his thoughts now. I don't want to see anyone's thoughts ever again.

I'm not sure how long I watch him. But I finally ask the question that has been bothering me.

"Why did you come get me?" I whisper, my voice croaking from disuse. I haven't said more than a few words in the past week. Not since I gave an official account of what happened.

Ikthiel studies me for a moment, choosing his words carefully perhaps. All he says is, "You're my friend."

"You could have died," I whisper back.

"So could you," he counters.

"It wouldn't have been enough before."

Ikthiel shakes his head. "It's funny how much we underestimated friendship," he says. "It's the greatest weapon in the universe. It's the reason we bend over backwards and put ourselves in danger. All in the name of some concept, some connection."

No answer comes to me. I'm not sure what to make of his assessment.

"Penelope, you're the reason I asked for the power. I wouldn't let the other demons harm you," he says. "They would have killed you for it."

Gently he brushes my cheek with his claws. How disconnected I feel from the younger version of myself afraid at the sight of his claws.

"You gave it to them?" I ask, remembering the price if he didn't.

"Yes," he whispers.

I understand what he says about friendship. His friendship is why I willingly gave power to him, power that could be used to kill or destroy. My desire to keep Ikthiel safe pushed me to do it. His life in danger was enough.

I reach up and put my hand over his, closing my eyes and feeling his power under his skin. The oddly comforting touch of the demon's unnatural power sitting just below the surface. I drift off again.

When I wake this time, Ikthiel is gone and Altair sits next to me. He looks up when I wake, sitting close in the chair as Ikthiel did.

"What happens now?" I ask softly. It's clearly daytime, but early. I don't want to wake anyone still sleeping.

Altair lets out a breath. "They are transferring you to another ship headed for Earth," he whispers. "You're going home."

I can't even muster enough energy to be surprised.

"Rebecca Whitney is dead," I say.

"Yes," he whispers. "But your mother agreed to terms to take you back in, now that . . ." his explanation drifts off.

"Now that she's alone," I whisper back. "Is that safe?"

"You'll be monitored," he says. "I'm sure Ikthiel will make appearances regularly, but so will Harilsen and Alicia and others." He adds, "You'll be given a direct teleport and a direct line of communication out just in case." He hesitates, pausing.

"What is it?" I ask.

"Your father has left Darien, as I understand it," Altair adds. "I don't think Alicia would be willing to send you if he were still close at hand."

I nod. "Darien is my mother's hometown, not his," I explain. "I'm assuming my brother went with him."

"I don't know," he says.

For a moment we just stare at each other. Then he continues, "After breakfast, Alicia wants to meet with you. She'll accompany you home."

The first person to want to meet with me in a week and it's Alicia Cole. "Alright," I say.

Altair sits back as the attendant healer looks around the divider. I sit up in bed and a table reminiscent of one I would see in an Earth hospital is rolled up to my bed. Altair steps out to give me space while I eat.

About an hour later Altair comes back to bring me to Alicia Cole. I haven't been out of the infirmary in a week, so I welcome the escort.

He takes me through corridors subtly curving up a gravity wheel, around to a section of offices and technical spaces. Down a tiny side hall, narrow doors tightly line each wall. We walk to the fourth one on the left and Altair presses a buzzer.

Rather than sliding back, the door simply vanishes, leaving a gap for us to step through. On the other side, the room is long and narrow, with no windows and only a semi-holographic screen on one wall. Around the screen and lining the office are what look like small compartments or lockers.

Alicia Cole sits at a desk built into one side wall, jutting out like a peninsula into the cramped room. Her back to the far wall, she looks up at us and smiles wanly in greeting. She taps the panel in front of her and the screen propped at a 45-degree angle drops into the desk and goes blank. She presses a ubiquitous section on the wall by her desk triggering two small chairs to pop out of the wall to our left.

"Please, have a seat. Both of you," she says, gesturing for us to take the chairs. Behind us the door reappears. The room, already small, feels stiflingly cramped with the three of us shoved in here.

To me, Alicia Cole says, "I understand Altair told you we are going back to Earth?"

I nod.

"Earth has a distinct shortage of Witches, as your history studies probably taught you," Alicia Cole continues. "With Rebecca Whitney's death, the only remaining Witches on Earth are in Europe and northern Asia."

"Which is why you reached out to my mother," I conclude for her, my voice cracking on the words.

"I'm afraid the only living relatives you have left are mostly on your father's side," Alicia Cole says. "Your mother seemed like the best option."

"You couldn't let me live with a friend?" I ask, thinking of Lucy and her emails still coming through to my communicator.

"If Earth knew about Witches publicly already, then it wouldn't be an issue," she explains. "There's too much risk in exposing them to a bigger understanding of the universe."

Internally, I feel she's misjudged the St. Johns. Being scientists, they must have considered alien life at least once. I don't feel I have a chance even if I argue. She's not wrong about how difficult it is to break the news to people who don't know. A chill goes up my spine remembering her in my living room, talking to my parents.

"What about Nahnu-beit?" I say suddenly, Fahum coming to mind.

"They weren't hit yet in the Kolvat attack, so yes they are still available," she acknowledges, "but there are no designated fosters there. It would take months to set one up, if anyone would volunteer." She pauses, glancing at Altair before adding, "The Rega family went through the process years ago. Few fosters take in humans."

Altair shifts next to me, his jaw clenched tight. He turns eighteen in a week and no longer requires a guardian at that point. I know he still intends to stay in touch with the surviving Rega family, the older siblings and Imfra-Rega's lifemate. It won't ever be the same again. Even now, without any contact between us, I feel the coil of grief wound tightly within him.

I look away from Alicia Cole. All I can do is shake my head and accept what is coming. Being fourteen has its drawbacks.

"There is one more thing."

My gaze returns to her. She leans forward, her elbows on the desk looking directly at me.

"We want you to be careful with your power," she says. "The Kolvat are still out there and they are attracted to it. Please restrain yourself, even while you continue to train."

Somehow the thought of using that much power while still on Earth is revolting. The idea of drawing down the Kolvat on my homeworld brings a shudder. There is no chance I would do that to Earth.

"Understood," is all I can think to say.

Satisfied, Alicia Cole leans back in her chair and pauses for a breath. Then she holds out her hand and asks for my wrist communicator. I unhook it and hand it over to her. She pulls up the settings and explains, "I'm overriding your usual restrictions and installing a recall. If for whatever reason it gets separated from you, it will return to your wrist." She hands back the communicator. "You'll be able to activate an emergency signal with a thought if necessary."

Tension fills my chest at the thought of what kind of emergency could make that necessary. I don't trust my mother. My only consolation is that my father doesn't live in Darien anymore. I let out a tight breath.

Alicia Cole's face softens. "I know this isn't ideal," she says. "I can't say how long the arrangement will be. But I can promise you'll have a visitor at least once a week, more if I know Ikthiel."

My mouth twitches and I snort.

Altair glances my way. "I'll come by too," he says.

"With limitations," Alicia Cole adds. "Now that the Kolvat are tracking your power as well."

Altair nods but doesn't say anything. It's hard to argue.

"Do you have any questions for me?" she asks.

I shake my head. I really don't. I feel hemmed in by my options.

"Well," she says, "contact me or find me if you do. We'll be leaving the ship in about two days."

Slowly, Altair gets up from his stool and I follow. Back in the hallway, the door reappears behind us and he leads us down to the main passage. Around the corner and a few feet from that path, Altair pauses. I look at him expectantly.

"I know she said they'll come running if you alert them," he says. "But really if anything happens either Ikthiel or I will come and get you, rules or no rules."

A shadow of a smile lifts the corners of my mouth. "You really mean that, don't you," is all I can think to say. It's not a question.

"Of course," he says. He stares at me standing there in the hallway. Abruptly, he reaches out and hugs me. I don't know how to react. Belatedly I reach my arms around him and remember what it is to hug another person.

As the hug lingers on, I realize it's not for me he is hugging me. Altair has been through more than any teenager should. Or any person, really. Eventually we all feel grief, but not like this. Not losing his home planet and family twice. This is different.

I don't know how long we stand in the hallway like that blocking the occasional passerby. But eventually Altair pulls back and we begin walking again. By this time I am worn out, still recovering as I am. Without a word, Altair takes my hand. In the infirmary again, Ikthiel is waiting in the chair by my bed. He rises when we come in, his eyes going to our hands I think. He takes my other one and the two help me back into bed.

For a moment I just stare at the flat ceiling of the infirmary.

My life out here among the stars is coming to an end it seems. I roll onto my side, Ikthiel tucking me in like before.

Sometime later I fall asleep again.


A few days later the medical cruiser has rendezvoused with the transport ship heading for Earth. I'm not sure if it will actually go to Earth or if we'll get close enough to do a low-power teleport. It almost doesn't matter.

What few belongings I have left are packed into a small bag that's light enough for me to carry without the healers looking concerned. Alicia Cole comes to get me from the infirmary and we walk through the maze of the ship to the airlock where the transport ship is docked.

There in the vestibule stand Altair, Ikthiel, and Firrl.

"We waited to bid you farewell," Firrl says. Silently she adds, *I will be coming to visit soon. I look forward to your oceans.*

I smile at her, a genuine, broad smile. Awkwardly I hug the tall fish, her personal ocean wetting my sleeve for a moment before cohering back into the suit. Oddly I find myself missing her lab.

*We will rebuild,* she says quietly to me.

Altair hugs me but doesn't say anything. We have already said our goodbyes. And it will not be long before he visits. As everyone seems to know by now, he and Ikthiel regularly visit me on Earth.

And Ikthiel smiles at me before giving me a tight embrace. The tiny demon spark flairs in response to his closeness, a feeling of controlled chaos I've grown familiar with in the past week. I'm not sure I'll ever be fully used to it, but then again I thought that about Ikthiel's claws too. The demon has turned into one of the most important people in my life.

So quietly I doubt any other could hear, he whispers in my ear, "Same for me."

The hug lingers for a bit before Alicia Cole coughs unceremoniously. Ikthiel pulls back and I step away from him. "I'll come as soon as I can," he says.

A smile curls the corners of my mouth. For a moment I look

at the faces of my friends, the few I have in this universe. Then Alicia Cole guides me through the medical cruiser's airlock and into the airlock on the other ship.

On the other ship, I turn back to see my friends standing there watching me go. Altair and Ikthiel and Firrl in the back. Ikthiel lifts a hand, his claws waving me off. I lift a hand and return the wave. The airlock shuts.

A few seconds later the ship detaches from the medical cruiser. Through the windows I watch them recede from view, quickly disappearing into the distance. Alicia Cole pulls me away to find our cabin.

The ship heads for Earth.

# EPILOGUE

## *AFTER*

In the afternoon on my walk home I tend to take a circuitous route, weaving through Darien like I am searching for buried treasure. After the vastness of space, this cramped town makes me feel claustrophobic. And it's funny to think that. In space I was always hemmed into corridors or stuck on ships or confined to a breathing unit at least. I never felt cramped though. I never felt claustrophobic.

Aside from the space and the light, the thing I miss the most are the clothes. I'm back with my mother and I'm wearing dresses and skirts again. The first weekend back she took me shopping for the first time in almost five years. Instead of an empty room bare of any semblance of life, she filled it with clothes and things she approved of. She let me choose but not choose. She gave me options and allowed no deviation from those choices. Between school uniforms and these clothes, not a hint of my magical life remains. At least my room is not bare anymore.

After everything that happened, I am ready for a rest from my bigger self.

The voice of Widdershin dying still echoes in my dreams.

Some days I go to the church and work with my mom. Mostly I do homework, but sometimes I'm roped into the church activities. I used to care about that kind of thing. It doesn't bother me anymore to be required to help out or participate. I've seen enough of the universe to know how it is, and fighting with ingrained beliefs feels exhausting after everything I've been through.

Today is one of those days when I take a few extra minutes to sit in the park. My books spread out on the picnic table before me, but really I'm just staring at the water and watching cars drive over the bridge. This first week back to school in the normal human world has been challenging.

"Penny? Is that you?"

I look up at the person coming closer. "Bryce," I say.

"May I sit?"

Bryce Christopherson, the son of the principle of McIntosh Middle, joins me at the table. It feels so strange to be talking to a completely normal human, and someone who doesn't know me very well at all.

"Lucy told me you were back," he says. "She's very excited."

"Yes, I talked to her yesterday," I answer. My mother has not allowed her over yet, but with my watchers keeping tabs on me, it is only a matter of time. I look down at my watch. I have to be at the church in fifteen minutes. "I have to go Bryce."

"Where are you headed?"

"Church," I say vaguely.

"Your mom's church?"

"Yeah."

"I can walk with you if you want," he offers.

I can't think of a reason to say no. So I just nod in assent and we both get up from the picnic table. Bryce gets a few steps ahead of me. His back is to me. I glance up to see Ikthiel on the bridge. He nods and gives a crooked smile, disappears again. He'll come back later.

Together Bryce and I walk down the street, under the trees of Darien.

I am in the company of humans again.

# ABOUT THE AUTHOR

Olivia "Lollie" Jones Black has been writing in some form or other since she was eleven. Her writing provides an emotional and creative outlet during this chaotic time. With work spanning a broad range of themes and worlds, she brings the reader to places both familiar and far away.

A background in science provides inspiration for her work. Her writing blends both science fiction and fantasy, epic and mundane. Genre matters less to her than the development of characters and story.

Her favorite author is the intrepid Diane Duane, who influenced her early love of science fiction-fantasy genre mixing.

A cat who thinks she owns the computer occasionally helps with the writing. She lives on the east coast.